PRAISE FOR
STREET JOURN/

JAN MORAN

Seabreeze Inn and Coral Cottage series

"A wonderful story… Will make you feel like the sea breeze is streaming through your hair." – Laura Bradbury, Bestselling Author

"A novel that gives fans of romantic sagas a compelling voice to follow." – *Booklist*

"An entertaining beach read with multi-generational context and humor." – *InD'Tale* Magazine

"Wonderful characters and a sweet story." – Kellie Coates Gilbert, Bestselling Author

"A fun read that grabs you at the start." – Tina Sloan, Author and Award-Winning Actress

"Jan Moran is the queen of the epic romance." —Rebecca Forster, *USA Today* Bestselling Author

"The women are intelligent and strong. At the core is a strong, close-knit family." — Betty's Reviews

The Chocolatier

"A delicious novel, makes you long for chocolate." – *Ciao Tutti*

"Smoothly written…full of intrigue, love, secrets, and romance." – *Lekker Lezen*

The Winemakers

"Readers will devour this page-turner as the mystery and passions spin out." – *Library Journal*

"As she did in *Scent of Triumph*, Moran weaves knowledge of wine and winemaking into this intense family drama." – *Booklist*

The Perfumer: Scent of Triumph

"Heartbreaking, evocative, and inspiring, this book is a powerful journey." – Allison Pataki, *NYT* Bestselling Author of *The Accidental Empress*

"A sweeping saga of one woman's journey through World War II and her unwillingness to give up even when faced with the toughest challenges." — Anita Abriel, Author of *The Light After the War*

"A captivating tale of love, determination and reinvention." — Karen Marin, Givenchy Paris

"A stylish, compelling story of a family. What sets this apart is the backdrop of perfumery that suffuses the story with the delicious aromas – a remarkable feat!" — Liz Trenow, *NYT* Bestselling Author of *The Forgotten Seamstress*

"Courageous heroine, star-crossed lovers, splendid sense of time and place capturing the unease and turmoil of the 1940s; HEA." — *Heroes and Heartbreakers*

BOOKS BY JAN MORAN

Summer Beach Series

Seabreeze Inn

Seabreeze Summer

Seabreeze Sunset

Seabreeze Christmas

Seabreeze Wedding

Seabreeze Book Club

Seabreeze Shores

Seabreeze Reunion

Seabreeze Honeymoon

Seabreeze Gala

Seabreeze Library

Coral Cottage Series

Coral Cottage

Coral Cafe

Coral Holiday

Coral Weddings

Coral Celebration

Coral Memories

Crown Island Series

Beach View Lane

Sunshine Avenue

Orange Blossom Way

The Love, California Series

Flawless

Beauty Mark

Runway

Essence

Style

Sparkle

20th-Century Historical

Hepburn's Necklace

The Chocolatier

The Winemakers: A Novel of Wine and Secrets

The Perfumer: Scent of Triumph

Life is a Cabernet

Seabreeze Gala

USA TODAY & WALL STREET JOURNAL BESTSELLING AUTHOR
JAN MORAN

SEABREEZE GALA

SUMMER BEACH, BOOK 10

JAN MORAN

SUNNY PALMS
PRESS

Library of Congress Cataloging-in-Publication Data
Moran, Jan.
/ by Jan Moran

ISBN 978-1-64778-189-7 (epub)
ISBN 978-1-64778-190-3 (paperback)
ISBN 978-1-64778-191-0 (hardcover)
ISBN 978-1-64778-192-7 (large print)
ISBN 978-1-64778-193-4 (audiobook)

Published by Sunny Palms Press. Cover design by Sleepy Fox Studios. Cover
images copyright Deposit Photos.

Sunny Palms Press
9663 Santa Monica Blvd STE 1158
Beverly Hills, CA, USA
www.sunnypalmspress.com
www.JanMoran.com

1

*C*arrying a vintage orange crate from the garage, Ivy opened the kitchen door with her sneaker, taking care to navigate around little Daisy, who was now crawling across the kitchen floor toward a shaft of sunlight on the linoleum.

Her sister Shelly was a relaxed beach mom who thought germs were a necessary part of life. Fortunately, they had just mopped.

Ivy plopped the box on the counter and rolled up her sleeves. "I found more decorations we might use for the fundraiser." She removed the dusty muslin fabric covering the former owner's party treasures they'd found.

Her younger sister and their niece traded a quick guilty glance.

Ivy knew that look. She waggled a finger between them. "What's up with you two?"

"Why do you always think that?" Shelly shot back. "Hey, slow down, Daisy-cakes." She swept back her tumbling chestnut hair, then scooped up her daughter and pointed her in a new direction away from the stove.

Ivy rubbed her neck, slightly exasperated at whatever secret they were keeping. "If there's something I should know, don't hold back. This gala will decide the fate of the Seabreeze Inn."

Poppy raised her brow. "Aunt Ivy, we think the event should be grand enough for wealthy donors to feel compelled to contribute to the restoration fund, but…"

"Not too spectacular," Shelly finished. "Or they'll think we don't need their help. Maybe we should let a few cracks in the façade show."

"No shortage of those." Grinning, Ivy pushed her hair from her forehead. "We could share photos of our antiquated plumbing and electrical systems. Better yet, let's put buckets under the leaky ceilings. Decorated, of course."

"That would be novel," Shelly said, chuckling. "But Viola might have a fit."

Ivy hooked her thumbs in the pockets of her workday blue jeans. "Look, anyone who's ever owned a home knows you can't patch and paint forever—especially a property of this age. Still, I want people to see what a magnificent historical property this is—and how much better it could be. It's for all of Summer Beach now, not only us."

For the past few years, she had been keeping the old beach house together with a combination of luck, fortitude, and quick fixes. But that recipe for marginal success wouldn't stretch much farther in a house now a hundred years old.

When Ivy arrived in Summer Beach, her goal had been to make the rooms comfortable enough to rent for income. Yet, the more she learned about the historical home, the more she felt drawn to restore the inn to its former glory as a center-piece of the community.

"Wow, would you look at this?" Poppy unwrapped a slightly dented silver serving dish blackened with age. "This place might be a little downtrodden, but I suppose guests from San Francisco and the Bay Area will expect an elegant affair. This piece should polish up well."

"That's what people say about us—right, Ives?" Shelly

laughed and plucked a purple feather boa from a different box. "Don't worry; fancy is my middle name. I have to wear this."

Ivy swatted her sister on the shoulder. "I'm serious. This is an ultra-black-tie fundraiser. You saw the invitations." They were creamy ivory with gold embossing that read: *The Las Brisas del Mar Historical Preservation Gala at the Seabreeze Inn.*

"How's this?" Shelly looped the long, fluffy strand around her neck.

"Don't you dare." They might not have a large budget, but Ivy was determined to welcome guests to the most glamorous beachside gala they could muster.

Guests would have to imagine how the old structure would look once renovated, but the inn had to shine with sparkling possibility. After all, that's what the fundraiser was for.

Ivy was incredibly grateful to Viola Standish for seeding the event with her generous donation. The auction of Amelia Erickson's newly discovered Victorian diamond necklace would be the highlight of the evening.

Nearby, Daisy gurgled with laughter. With surprising speed, she crawled in wide-eyed wonder toward twin turquoise refrigerators humming like a Pied Piper. She stared, fixated, on the lower grate, which concealed all sorts of dangers.

"Watch out, Daisy alert," Poppy called out.

"Gotcha." Shelly swooped down to lift Daisy, now a chubby hands-width from another potential disaster. "Relax, I've got this, Ives. With this fabulous bit of finery and a black sundress, I'm ready for anything." Daisy grabbed the feather boa with glee.

Ivy wasn't so sure. "We must be at the top of our game, or Viola will be extremely disappointed. She committed to inviting her friends, who all have very high standards. You are not wearing a faded old sundress—with or without that tragic purple thing."

Shelly grinned. "Don't worry. I'll find a sparkly dress. We

still need to figure out what we're wearing. How about Thrifty Threads? That will fit into our budgets."

"It will have to." Ivy laughed, but she liked that idea. "It's just one evening anyway."

She'd been so busy tending to the gala preparations that she hadn't had time to think about a dress. Viola would expect her and Shelly to be properly attired to greet her guests.

Viola had strict standards.

A few months ago, Ivy and Bennett's honeymoon flight was delayed in San Francisco. They sought out the old Erickson home and met the current owner, Viola Standish, and her niece, Meredith. The Pacific Heights house was spectacular. Amelia Erickson had engaged the same architect to build her summer home, Las Brisas del Mar, which Ivy had christened the Seabreeze Inn. Both properties carried historical designations.

Viola referred to Ivy and herself as custodians of history. The Seabreeze Inn had become more than an inn; it was a frequent gathering place for Summer Beach residents. Everyone was welcome to roam art shows on the grounds and attend the annual holiday festivities. The inn also hosted book clubs, and music students visited to practice and perform. The old beach house inn buzzed with locals and guests alike.

Considering all this, Viola's nonprofit organization and her advisor helped Ivy apply for a combination of grants, tax credits, and other creative options to provide funds for repairs. Viola's standards for historical preservation were high.

Shelly tickled Daisy's face with the feathers. "I can do high standards all day long. I made about a billion floral arrangements for bridezillas and charity mavens in New York. For this event, I envision a glamorous, vintage seafaring theme of aquamarine blue and seafoam green with silver accents. Let's play up the old beach house angle."

"We could check with Arthur at Antique Times," Poppy

said. "Maybe he would lend us the old ship's wheel and buoys in the window for the event."

Shelly's eyes brightened. "Great idea. The old ballroom will sparkle with treasures, I promise."

"It has to." Ivy opened another box. "This is it. If we don't raise enough money to repair everything here, we'll be looking for other jobs." At least the ballroom was in reasonably good shape with its vintage chandeliers, comfortably worn parquet floors, and an enormous fireplace. Low lights would soften the imperfections.

Still, a growing construction list loomed in Ivy's mind. The old grand dame by the sea needed repairs or replacements to the roof, windows, insulation, electrical, plumbing, heating, and air-conditioning.

If Ivy had extra funds, she would continue restoring the hardwood floors and other interior features. The only part that didn't need substantial work was the surrounding garden. Shelly had already worked her horticultural magic on the grounds, though Ivy suspected Shelly had a wish list, too.

Poppy hefted another old orange crate to the counter. "This is the last of the decorations. I hope there's a lot we can repurpose. Wow, lots of old seashells in here." She wrinkled her brow at the gaudy feather boa. "But maybe not that thing, Aunt Shelly. Surely you can do better than that."

"I'll consider that a throwdown. And I can use all those shells. We can't take them from the beach anymore." Shelly unwound the boa, plucking purple feathers from her shoulders and Daisy's soft blond curls.

They all laughed. Her sister was creative; Ivy would give her that. They had both inherited that trait from their mother, who was somewhere on the other side of the world sailing the high seas with their father. Even in their seventies, their parents were out living their best lives and showed few signs of slowing down, physically or mentally. *Goals*, Ivy thought, smiling to herself.

She was figuring out how to live her best life, too. Memories of her honeymoon with Bennett in Mallorca floated to mind. Her mother had been right about that being an essential trip for them. It was the most time they'd ever spent together, just the two of them. Ivy would cherish those recollections as long as she lived.

She leaned on the countertop, surveying the assortment of glittery decorations. "I could sure use Mom's advice right now. Remember all the parties she and Dad used to throw?"

Shelly plucked another feather from her T-shirt and tickled Daisy's nose. The little girl laughed and clapped her hands. "They loved to entertain. I remember sneaking out of bed to watch the grownups and snitch all the desserts I could carry back to my room."

"We all did." Ivy smiled. "Won't be long before Daisy is doing that, too."

Her tiny niece had started crawling with gusto and pulling up to stand. She was babbling nearly nonstop. Soon, she'd be walking and forming coherent words. It seemed like only yesterday that her daughters were that age. Those days flew by in a seemingly endless whirlwind of laundry, dishes, and sleepless nights.

Her daughters were grown now. Sunny was poised to graduate from university this year. Misty worked as an actress in Los Angeles, steadily paying her dues with commercials, audiobooks, theater, and small television parts. Ivy knew her break would come soon.

Intrigued by the finery on the counters, Daisy tried to squirm out of Shelly's arms.

"Daisy is going to be outrunning us soon. We'll need to keep up." Ivy was closer to being a grandmother than a young mother again. That thought shocked her. She had been Misty's age when her first child was born.

The house phone trilled, banishing that thought, and Ivy

picked up the extension in the kitchen. "It's a sunny day at the Seabreeze Inn. How may I help you?"

A strong, authoritative voice burst through the receiver. "This is Mrs. Hampshire. I'm calling to make a reservation for Viola Standish's charity gala."

Ivy shook her head. She wished she could conjure more rooms. "I'm sorry, but we're fully booked. You could try the Seal Cove Inn or a hotel in a neighboring town."

"Would you recheck your reservations? I can assure you that I will make it worth your while. I'm sure your rates will be much higher, if you know what I mean."

"I don't need to check, and we haven't raised our rates for that week."

Mrs. Hampshire let out a labored sigh. "I will offer you a bonus of five thousand dollars. You don't have to tell your boss about it. Simply cancel someone else's reservation. But not Viola or Meredith, of course. Tell the other guest you had a plumbing leak or something. And I want the room next to Viola."

The woman spoke so loudly that her voice reverberated through the kitchen. Shelly gave her an enthusiastic thumbs-up.

Pressing her lips together, Ivy shook her head. "Ma'am, I am the boss, and we're still fully reserved. However, I am happy to add your name to the waiting list."

Shelly smacked a hand to her forehead and rolled her eyes.

Mrs. Hampshire continued, "I could buy that place, you know."

Some had tried; Ivy bit back a comment. "I wish I could accommodate you, truly I do. We have a limited number of rooms." She jotted the woman's contact information on a notepad by the phone. "I look forward to seeing you at the gala."

After she hung up, Shelly made a face. "She was right. I

don't know why we're not charging a premium for rooms that week. Still, it's a good thing I didn't take that call. On that last suggestion, I would have told her where to—"

Poppy cut in, "It's a good thing Aunt Ivy is diplomatic."

Shelly feigned innocence. "Where to find another lodging, I meant to say. Why do you two think I always give attitude?"

"Because you do." Even though Shelly's sharp banter had gotten them in trouble on more than one occasion, Ivy loved her sister.

Poppy held up a strand of seashells and a pair of long silver tassels. "We could use these in the ballroom."

"They'd look great on the mantle." Ivy brought out another pair.

"You're not even listening to me," Shelly said. "We could have doubled our rates for that week. Maybe we still could."

Ivy narrowed her eyes in warning. "It's too late now. We should have thought about that before the first reservation came in."

The first person to reserve a room was Lea Martin from Europe. She had made her reservation within minutes of the press release going out. Ivy assumed she was a friend of Viola's, but the woman didn't know her.

"They have to stay somewhere, and this is the prime place." Shelly wasn't letting up. "But seriously, where do you think people stayed back when Amelia threw her grand parties in the ballroom?"

"I never thought about that," Ivy replied. "Maybe they drove from Los Angeles or San Diego."

"Or had their chauffeurs do the driving," Poppy added.

"That's more likely." Ivy could imagine that. After all, she lived in the Erickson's old chauffeur's quarters above the garage. "Wasn't there a photo of the chauffeurs playing cards while they waited in one of those old photo journals we found?"

Poppy snapped her fingers. "We should check out the old photos to see how Amelia decorated for parties back then."

"That's a good idea," Ivy said.

"I'll get the photo albums." Poppy hurried from the kitchen.

Easing onto a stool at the counter, Ivy faced her sister. "Come on, Shells. We've got to make sure everything runs smoothly for this event. No antagonizing or fleecing the guests, please. You know how much this means to all of us."

Shelly tousled Daisy's curls. "Just chill, Ives. I'll behave, I promise. I do know how."

"You just choose not to."

"Where's the fun in doing what's expected of you all the time?" She flung the boa around her shoulders, tucked Daisy under her arms, and flounced from the kitchen, throwing back an excuse. "Have to change Daisy's diaper now."

Ivy passed a hand over her forehead, though she couldn't help but smile. Her sister always did things her way. Ivy had been accused of that, too.

That wasn't surprising, though; they were both their mother's daughters.

Just then, the rear door opened, and her husband stepped inside. With his broad shoulders and closely cropped, sun-streaked hair, Bennett could still make her heart race. "You're home early."

"I had some business in town and finished early." He took her in his arms and kissed her. "Still up for our date night?"

Although a dozen things still needed to be done around the inn, Ivy nodded. Having date nights was one of the pledges they'd made to each other on their honeymoon. Decoration plans could wait, but spending promised time with her husband couldn't.

To that end, she had delegated the cleaning of rooms to a part-time housekeeper and the accounting to a bookkeeper. Getting the inn up and running had required enormous effort and sacrifice, but now that the occupancy level had increased, she could ease off a little. The last few years had been an emotional rollercoaster filled with challenges. Now, she was trying to pace herself and lead a more balanced life.

However, like Shelly, life didn't always oblige. "Did you have anything in mind for tonight?"

Bennett thought for a moment. "We could put the top down on the old Chevy and cruise the beach. Maybe stop for takeout and watch the moon come up."

"Only if you bring your guitar." She knew her daughter was studying late with a friend, and Poppy had told her she had a date with a new man she'd met. Ivy and Shelly were dying to know more, but Poppy wouldn't give up details.

"I'll put it in the car right now. I know just the spot."

Poppy reappeared with an old photo album they had found in the house. She held it open to a spread of sepia photographs. "They sure knew how to dress back then. Amelia's parties look amazing."

"We were working on the gala decorations," Ivy said to Bennett, sweeping a hand across the colorful mess.

Bennett glanced around the kitchen. "I can see that."

Poppy placed the old photo album on the kitchen table, and they gathered around. "Amelia decorated the mantle like we were talking about. But look at these slinky evening gowns." She squinted at them. "They could be in style today. Elena's fashion designer friend Fianna Fitzgerald created similar styles in her current collection."

"And the jewelry is incredible." Ivy cradled her chin, wondering if their attendees would turn up in such finery. Poppy's cousin, Elena, a successful jewelry designer in Los Angeles, was her older sister Honey's daughter. Poppy still helped Elena and Fianna with marketing campaigns.

Poppy tilted her head. "Viola did put black-tie on the invitation."

"What do you plan on wearing?" Bennett asked Ivy.

"Shelly and I are going shopping." She shrugged, happy to make the best of their limited budget. "Nothing that glamorous, though. We're basically the help."

Bennett's eyebrows shot up. "You're a business owner, the hostess, and the mayor's wife, don't forget."

"I won't embarrass you, darling." Ivy smoothed a hand over Bennett's shoulder. "But I can't compete with Viola's old money friends. Besides, the whole point is to raise funds for the inn. If we look like we don't need assistance, what kind of message will that send?"

Poppy twisted her lips to one side. "But you don't have to look shabby, Aunt Ivy."

"Now you sound like your grandmother," Ivy said. Years of travel had honed Carlotta Reina Bay's unique sense of style, whether she wore a flowing beach skirt or a chic ensemble for the opera.

Bennett put her arm around her. "Poppy has a point. Now, about that drive we were talking about…"

"Let's look at these photos tomorrow," Ivy said. "You can show me your favorites."

Bennett kissed Ivy's cheek. "I'll get my guitar. Do you have your keys?"

Patting her pocket, she said, "I'll meet you at the car."

Ivy plucked a lightweight windbreaker from a hook beside the rear door and draped it around her shoulders. She walked to the garage to pull out the vintage, cherry-red Chevy that had once belonged to Amelia and Gustav. Bennett had restored it beautifully for her. She put the top down and smoothed her hand over the broad steering wheel, wondering about the adventures this old car had seen.

One incident came to mind.

While cleaning the attic, she and Shelly found a page torn from a journal that Amelia had written. The poor woman described her anger and dismay when she'd become lost on an outing in Summer Beach. She was turned around, heading up the coast toward Los Angeles instead of down the coast toward San Diego. She chastised herself, writing that she should have noticed the ocean was on the wrong side.

Ivy figured that was when her Alzheimer's disease was becoming more apparent. Her driver insisted that he drive her from then on, but Amelia clearly loved and missed her independence.

When she heard the door to their apartment over the garage slam, she slid across the bench seat to the passenger side and flipped down the visor mirror to refresh her lip gloss.

Since she and Bennett had returned from their honeymoon in Mallorca, Ivy had been working on their marriage, putting themselves first as they'd promised each other. Even though they both had demanding work, they now made a point to take time for themselves. That might only be a walk on the beach after work, a glass of wine at sunset, or a late-night chat in their tree-sheltered balcony, but they were together.

Now that Poppy ran most of the afternoon wine and tea greetings for guests, Ivy used that time to paint. It was such a relief to escape for a couple of hours to work. The gallery owner in Sausalito had already sold some of her Summer Beach and Mallorca paintings she'd been able to finish.

While painting might be her true calling, she loved running the inn, too. She had come so close to selling it a few months ago and was glad she hadn't. The old beach house provided her family with a home, income, and a steady stream of guests who kept life interesting.

Sometimes, Bennett would entertain in the evening by the firepit, strumming his guitar for guests for a little while. They always retired early, leaving their guests to chat for the rest of the night if they wished.

"Let's hit the road." Bennett placed his guitar case in the back seat before sliding behind the wheel. "I feel like we're running away, but I love it. And I love you." He kissed her cheek before starting the car.

She knew just how he felt. Old habits were hard to break. "We have a busy week ahead."

Bennett started the car and pulled from the courtyard onto the road. "You have a good team."

"Sunny seems busy, though."

"How are her classes going?"

"She's on track to graduate in May." After Sunny's mishap last semester, where her boyfriend stole and submitted her paper as his own, she'd been taking her schoolwork more seriously. "I think the threat of being expelled and losing her degree sank in, so she's determined to graduate now."

Bennett steered the car toward town. "I've noticed that, too. Handling the expulsion issue by herself gave Sunny a boost of confidence. She's capable of solving problems."

"That was an enormous step for her." Sunny's father had always rescued her, but admittedly, so had Ivy at times. Jeremy had simply thrown more money at her, but neither of them had done her any favors by doing that. Yet, when Sunny wailed and carried on, it was hard not to help her. Where did parents draw the line? There was no manual, no hard rules. What worked for one child was different for another.

"Thank goodness Sunny is finally growing up." Ivy bit her lip, realizing the onus wasn't only on her daughter. "I suppose we all are, except when you're an adult, it's called growing older and wiser. Do you think we are?"

Bennett chuckled as he parked in front of a new restaurant in town. "Older? That's a privilege. Wiser? Sure hope so."

"I haven't tried this one yet," Ivy said.

Summer Beach was attracting many new businesses to fill vacancies in the village. This was a result of Bennett's campaign to attract new entrepreneurs and help others stay in the community and flourish. The town offered a package of free and subsidized services.

Bennett opened the door for Ivy, and she got out. "Ocean View Cafe. A fusion of fresh California and Pacific Rim cuisine. Something smells delicious."

They stepped inside, and the owner acknowledged them with a friendly wave. "Your takeout is almost ready, Mayor."

Bennett approached the young woman, who welcomed them with a dazzling smile. "I'd like you to meet my wife, Ivy. She runs the Seabreeze Inn."

"And we have a lot of hungry guests," Ivy added. "Everyone in town has been wondering what would go in this space."

"We're in our soft opening phase." The proprietor, Hallie, showed them around the small restaurant, only a few doors from Java Beach, the coffee shop Shelly's husband owned. "We're training people and working out issues before our grand opening."

Ivy gazed at the handwritten menu on a chalkboard and turned to Bennett. "Looks very good. What did you order?"

"An assortment of dumplings and sushi. I thought you'd like the crab and avocado specialties."

She tucked her arm through his. "You know me pretty well."

"Hey, you two." A familiar voice rang out, and Ivy turned to see Megan and Josh, the documentary filmmakers who had bought a home in Summer Beach.

"We saw your car out front," Megan said. "Wow, the menu here looks fabulous. Mango curry soup, fresh catch, and homemade raspberry chocolate ice cream. I can't decide where to start."

"I'll bring samples," Hallie said, and she disappeared into the kitchen.

"I can hardly wait to meet Viola Standish," Megan said. "I hope she'll consent to an interview."

Ivy recalled her conversation with the older woman in San

Francisco. "You'll have to frame it as a service to Amelia's works and history."

Megan nodded thoughtfully. "Even if she refuses, I hope she can fill in the blanks in the Erickson's timeline and history. As much work as I've done, I still feel like we're missing parts of the puzzle, even after your discoveries in Mallorca."

"We were surprised," Ivy said. "If I hadn't stopped in to talk to Teresa at Get Away Travel or a fellow passenger on the flight hadn't acted up, we wouldn't have discovered any of that."

On the island, Ivy and Bennett had met a woman at a train station whose grandfather had known Amelia and her father in Berlin. Raquel shared a few details about how they managed to rescue important artwork otherwise condemned to burn. Still, the information was sparse.

Megan's eyes flashed with excitement. "The art angle is excellent and follows your discoveries at the inn, but I want to know more about their humanitarian work. There's a lot we still don't know. If only we could find her complete journals."

"Instead of page by page, right?" Amelia had often torn sheets from her journal and hidden them. But then, she had lived through tumultuous times, and with the onset of her illness, one had to forgive her eccentricities.

"I hope Viola is willing to talk to me this time," Megan said.

Bennett inclined his head. "Once you get to know her, she's quite the storyteller. You'll probably find no better source on Amelia Erickson."

Megan's grin widened. "That's what I'm counting on. I have so many questions; I want to ask her about all the loose ends you've found at the inn."

As the filmmaker's enthusiasm bubbled, Ivy's curiosity swelled. Somehow, Amelia's presence was still part of the old house, along with remnants of a life steeped in mystery and rich with untold stories.

As they spoke, Hallie brought out several tidbits for them to sample.

"This is heavenly; I have to order this." Megan sipped the mango curry soup from a small sample cup.

"Let's get an assortment," her husband Josh said.

While he ordered, Megan turned to Ivy. "I'd love to peel back the layers of Amelia's history. I know viewers will want to understand the woman who is as much a part of the inn as the weathered shingles and creaky floorboards."

"So do I," Ivy said. "Amelia is such an enigma. I've always wondered what drove her and what other secrets she kept locked away. Maybe we'll never fully grasp the intricacies of her life, but it's clear she loved her Las Brisas del Mar home."

"And now you'll carry it into a new era," Megan said.

Ivy hoped so, but after tallying the costs, the need was great. "As long as we raise enough for repairs and restoration."

"I'm sure you will." Excitement lit Megan's face. "When we unravel and bring the past to life, people feel more connected to it."

"More than that," Ivy said. "Learning their stories is like touching a piece of our souls. The tapestry of our lives is woven from the threads of those who came before us."

Megan's eyes rounded, and she reached for her phone. "I have to capture that thought," she said, tapping the screen. "Anything else to add?"

Ivy laughed. "Ask me later." She had grown to feel a deep connection to Amelia, not only on the art level but also on the personal, human level.

Hallie slid a pair of bags across the counter toward Bennett. "Your order is ready. We put a little extra inside. I hope you like it."

"I'm sure we will. Let me or my office know if you want to arrange a ribbon cutting and grand opening. Summer Beach residents are welcoming and supportive."

"Except for a few," Ivy said. "But don't let them scare you.

They're actually good-hearted."

"We're counting on that," Hallie said. "See, we're starting over. My husband's parents retired here from Seattle. After we lost everything in a hurricane in Houston, we wanted to be close to them and my folks. The community's programs have already been a great help."

"I'm happy to hear that," Bennett said.

Something in his voice struck Ivy as odd, but she let it go.

After leaving, Ivy tucked their takeout on the bench seat between them, and Bennett started the car. She brushed her hair back in the balmy ocean breeze, enjoying the fresh air. The ocean was calm tonight, and waves swept to shore with a mesmerizing rhythm.

"Where to, Mr. Mayor?"

"I thought we'd go up on the ridge. It's clear, so the view should be amazing. We can watch the stars come out."

"Lover's Peak, you mean?" Ivy smiled. That took her back a few years.

Bennett laughed. "It's a school night, so we'll probably be alone."

They drove the short distance in comfortable silence, passing Bennett's house on the way. The lights were on, and through the living room window, they could see a young family dancing in front of the television.

Ivy remembered doing the same with her daughters at that age. "Looks like your new tenant has settled in."

"I was lucky to find them." He pulled to a stop at the end of the street. In the gathering twilight, the lights of Summer Beach twinkled to life. "This reminds me of the old drive-in theater that used to be in Summer Beach."

Ivy liked that thought. "Only we're watching the sunset."

She opened the bags and spread the food between them. They talked as they ate, sharing the new dishes they liked. Simple as this date night was, Ivy loved being together, wherever they were.

They chatted about the upcoming gala as the sun sank toward the horizon, painting the sky with broad strokes of pink and gold. Their conversation was pleasant enough, yet she sensed something was weighing on her husband.

When Bennett finished his dumplings and sticky rice, Ivy cleared her throat. "Is there anything on your mind you'd like to talk about?"

"You know me too well." Bennett paused to sip water from a bottle. "There are whispers in town that Wyatt Snowden plans to run against me."

Ivy was surprised. "Is he a serious contender?"

"Apparently so. I didn't think so, but he's been railing against city programs designed to bring new small businesses to town, like Hallie's new restaurant."

"Surely people in Summer Beach support local businesses. He shouldn't have a chance against you."

Tilting his head back, Bennett stared up at the sky. "Maybe he does. He hasn't officially entered the race, but he has a lot of family money behind him."

"But he's against everything you're doing to keep Summer Beach as it is. He's trying to keep people out."

"Except for the big developers, it seems. As some residents move or pass on, the town needs the right growth and revital-ization, not the kind large developers bring. Not to this community."

Ivy folded her arms. "We'll see. I don't believe he can beat you."

Bennett passed a hand over his face and turned to her. Taking her hand, he looked into her eyes. "Would you still love me even if I was voted out?"

"Like we talked about on our honeymoon, everything changes." Yet, even as Ivy spoke, she had an unsettling feeling about Wyatt Snowden.

"Unfortunately, there is something else," Bennett said slowly. "And I wanted you to hear it from me first."

2

*I*vy stared at Bennett, noticing the consternation on his face. She wrapped her light jacket tighter around her shoulders, bracing herself.

"People are talking right now," Bennett began, his voice carrying a weight that immediately put Ivy on edge. "Some are asserting that I've been channeling city funds elsewhere. I believe the accusation is coming from Wyatt Snowden and his group. He hasn't even entered the race, and already it's getting ugly. The Java Beach crowd is talking."

"That's ridiculous." Ivy saw a warning in his gaze. "Where do they think you're diverting funds?"

Bennett ran a hand through his hair. "That's where this involves you."

"Me?"

"Supposedly, I'm taking funds from the city to support the inn."

"Where would people get such an idea?" Anger raced through her, and she searched Bennett's face for an explanation.

"They make them up," Bennett said. "I imagine Wyatt will

say people in the community are raising the question in order to call for an investigation and raise doubt. It's a classic move."

Ivy picked at a string on her jeans. "Is there anything they could find that might implicate you?"

Bennett shook his head. "I've tried to think of what could have been misconstrued, but there's nothing. Except for the time Boz and I brought the city management team to the inn for our annual brainstorming and planning session."

"I remember that." Her husband liked to take his team away from City Hall to minimize interruptions. They sequestered themselves in the dining room to get their work done.

He laced his hands over the steering wheel. "You ordered snacks from Java Beach. I insisted on paying you back with a check drawn on a Summer Beach account. That's a normal expense, and it was fairly minor. That's the only thing I know of that could be brought into question. Wyatt is insinuating cash payments, of course."

"But there was nothing like that." Ivy was incensed at the injustice of it all.

"Doesn't matter. By then, the damage will be done. Doubts will have been planted in people's minds, and the charge is sure to grow."

"I'm sure you can counter that claim and show Wyatt for the rat he is."

"Believe me, I'll try to make light of it." Bennett ran a hand over his hair. "But I have to be careful. Sometimes, if you deny things too loudly, people think you're covering up."

Ivy's heart raced. This charge was ludicrous, yet the potential damage these rumors could cause was all too real.

Their appetites had waned, so she wrapped up the remaining food. "This is absurd, Bennett. There must be something we can do."

"If I think of anything, I'll let you know. But you need to be prepared if people question you."

"I have nothing to hide."

Ivy sat in silence, grappling with the potential ramifications of Wyatt Snowden's tactics and how they might affect the inn and the upcoming gala.

She rubbed her forehead, considering the ugly rivalries in Bennett's profession. She hadn't thought that could happen in Summer Beach.

Another thought occurred to her. "Why does Wyatt want the position of mayor so badly?"

After hesitating, Bennett replied, "It's certainly not for the paycheck."

That was true; Summer Beach's budget was small, though adequate. Her husband still ran his real estate business with the help of another agent. "If Wyatt wanted glory, other communities could offer a lot more."

"I'm sure he has his reasons." He shook his head. "We've had developers who wanted to develop large commercial projects. We also have large municipal projects on which we take bids. Wyatt might see a chance to make significant money on the side. Bribery and kickbacks are not ethical or legal, but sadly, often done."

Ivy crossed her arms. "Well, I don't like his methods. I don't want to see you hurt."

Bennett kissed her softly. "And I don't want to involve you. Your attention needs to be on the gala, not meaningless rumors."

"They're only meaningless if there's no harm done."

"That's true." Bennett stretched his arm across the seat and gathered her close.

Ivy snuggled next to him, enjoying the warmth of his body next to hers. Surely, they could figure this out.

They watched the sun send a slow-motion riot of red streamers across the sky. Ivy drew a breath. She never tired of watching the day come to a dramatic close. The more clouds in the sky, the more spectacular the sunset.

Bennett turned and kissed her. "Ready to put all that behind us?"

"I'm ready for anything," she replied, whether she was or not. She was sure they hadn't heard the last of this Wyatt character, and she wondered how low he would stoop.

The drive back to the Seabreeze Inn was quiet, with each of them lost in their thoughts. Ivy felt a mix of anger and helplessness.

Bennett's reluctance to discuss the seriousness of the charges spoke volumes about his own turmoil. She knew he feared that rumors could tarnish not only his reputation but also affect the inn and their lives together.

Upon their return, the lively ambiance of the inn lifted her spirits a little. They had a late check in, and Ivy greeted the guests. They were excited to visit Summer Beach, and she enjoyed talking to them, although the ugly rumor nipped at her mind.

That night, she lay awake, staring at the ceiling as she listened to Bennett's steady breathing. The darkness of the room seemed to mirror the cloud of uncertainty that had settled over them.

The whispers of gossip, the insidious, false accusations, and the potential fallout disturbed Ivy. She grew more irritated at Wyatt Snowden for his baseless claims and at people so eager to indulge in scandalous gossip. She'd thought most people here were their friends. Plus, it was all over the gossip wire at Mitch's place.

Worst of all, the Seabreeze Inn, her labor of love and dedication, now stood in the shadow of suspicion.

While dawn broke and Bennett slipped out for his morning beach run, Ivy's resolve hardened. She would not let gossip define them or dictate their future.

. . .

Ivy marched into the kitchen, where Shelly stood by the sink, her hands buried in sudsy water. She stopped beside her.

Shelly's eyebrows shot up. "Oh, hey, Ives."

"Did Mitch tell you about the rumors swirling around Bennett and the inn?" Ivy picked up a dish towel to dry the large serving platters that didn't fit into the dishwasher.

Shelly's expression was a mixture of surprise and guilt.

"Always come to me first." Ivy whipped a towel across the platter and set it down.

"He heard the rumor at Java Beach. I didn't know how to tell you," Shelly added, her eyes not meeting Ivy's. "I thought if I ignored it, it might just go away. I didn't want to add to your stress over the gala."

"Stress? This is our livelihood we're talking about, Shells. Our reputation. Bennett's career. You thought keeping me in the dark would help?"

Shelly flinched, the criticism striking a nerve. "I was trying to protect you. The last thing you needed was more worry."

Ivy inclined her head; she'd give her sister that. "Have you met Wyatt?"

"No, but Mitch told me he and his election team have been rallying support at Java Beach."

Election team. So they were serious. "Knowing that would get back to us right away, I'm sure. I need you to have my back, to warn me about storms coming our way." Ivy's voice broke. "It's not only the inn. It's Bennett. He would never divert city funds here, and I would never accept them."

Shelly's eyes filled with tears, the realization of her mistake dawning on her. "Ivy, I'm so sorry." She hugged Ivy. "I thought I was doing the right thing, but I should have told you immediately."

"No more secrets?"

"I promise."

Ivy hugged Shelly back. "Now, hand me that other platter,

and let's knock out these breakfast dishes. We have a lot more planning to do."

In the sun-drenched parlor of the Seabreeze Inn, Ivy and Shelly huddled together on a plush sofa, an old leather-bound photo album sprawled across their laps. The sound of ocean waves crashed in the distance. The scent of salt air mingled with the heady scent of Shelly's tuberose stalks in the foyer.

Poppy, notebook in hand, perched on the edge of an adjacent armchair, her pen poised and ready. She'd already prepared notes this morning while Ivy and Shelly were busy.

Ivy carefully turned the album's brittle pages, revealing a black-and-white photograph of the beach house ballroom, decked out for an ocean beach-themed gala.

She paused, studying the details. The image was a snapshot in time, the elegance and grandeur of the era captured in the intricate details of the decor. Streamers that mimicked undulating waves hung from the ceiling, while tables were adorned with floral centerpieces flanked with coral, seashells, and starfish, faintly illuminated by candlelight.

Poppy tucked her silky blond hair behind an ear. "What do you think of that look?"

"Can you imagine walking into this?" Ivy whispered, her voice tinged with awe. "The Ericksons sure knew how to throw parties back then."

Shelly leaned closer, scanning the photograph. "It's breathtaking. The attention to detail is amazing. It's like stepping into another world."

"Look at this note," Poppy said. "'An undersea fantasy.'"

Ivy pointed to a corner of the image where a bandstand was set up, complete with a grand piano and brass instruments. "Live music was such a big part of these events. It brought everything to life."

"We'll have that." Ivy had already booked a group of musicians that specialized in period jazz and swing tunes. Furrowing her brow, Poppy scribbled in her notebook. "Do you think we could recreate that look? I could have these photos enlarged on easels. That would be a nice tribute to the original theme."

"I still like the captain's wheel idea." Ivy had called Arthur at Antique Times, and he was happy to lend whatever they might need.

She turned the page, revealing another photo of elegantly dressed guests, their faces bright with joy and laughter. "This is what we need to aim for—that sense of joy and community. It's not just about the decorations or the music. It's about creating an experience, a memory that will last."

Poppy nodded, her notes now filled with sketches and bullet points. "I'll research more."

"Chef Marguerite at Beaches will supply retro appetizers and cocktails," Ivy said. "That will add to the ambiance."

"I could also call Kai and Axe," Shelly said. "They might have vintage costumes at the theater we can borrow for servers and staff. Didn't people wear hats and scarves back then? That might be clever."

After gleaning what they could on how Amelia Erickson had once decorated, Shelly walked to the adjoining foyer. "We'll have a grand floral arrangement here to greet guests. Tuberose is impressive and dazzles the senses. I'll use a lot more, with lots of tropical flowers, greenery, shells, and drift-wood to give an impression of abundance."

"Curly willows would add height," Ivy suggested. "We could stain them or accent them with glitter."

"I'll see," Shelly said, motioning to Poppy. "I can wrap this banister with vintage decorations and greenery. Maybe I'll create an archway into the ballroom."

Ivy led the way into the vast space, where they had hosted

many weddings and local events. But the gala needed to be even more spectacular.

Poppy jotted a few more notes. "This is so exciting. Should we start decorating before the first guests arrive? The woman from Germany is arriving early."

"We should," Ivy replied. "Did we ever find out if she's a friend of someone's or a collector?"

"No idea who she is," Poppy said. "I asked Viola and Meredith, too."

"She might be an important collector," Ivy said. "Someone who would have been watching for auctions like this."

Poppy tapped her pen. "Besides Viola and Meredith, Lea Martin was the first to call for a reservation after I posted the press release. The invitations were still in the mail."

Shelly gazed up at the chandeliers, wrinkling her nose at the cobwebs. "Maybe she's a journalist covering the story."

"What do we know about the other guests?" Ivy asked.

"Only what they've shared with me," Poppy replied. "But I can do some research so that we don't embarrass ourselves."

Ivy nodded in agreement. "Viola will want all her guests treated like royalty."

"Then we'd better have the chandeliers cleaned," Shelly said, swiping at the cobwebs. "It's been a month since we've used this room. The little critters move in fast."

"On it," Poppy said, adding to her list.

Ivy gestured to another side of the room. "We'll need to bring up the tables from storage and have the tablecloths starched and pressed at the Laundry Basket. We can arrange the long tables for the silent auction, with a special place of honor for Amelia's necklace."

Poppy nodded with enthusiasm. "Maybe cover it with glass and illuminate it."

"I know how to do that," Shelly said. "I've helped people

do all sorts of things at events. Who knew all that random knowledge would come in handy again?"

Ivy smiled. "Mom always says knowledge is never wasted."

"I wish Mom and Dad could be here for this." A touch of sadness edged Shelly's voice. "Daisy sure misses the grandies."

So did Ivy. She touched her sister's shoulder. "We'll talk to them when they reach the next port."

A silence settled among them as Ivy thought about Carlotta and Sterling, who had left before she and Bennett departed on their honeymoon. Her parents usually checked in when they reached port. Ivy tried not to worry about them because they were doing what they loved. This challenging around-the-world trip was likely their last, though not the end of their sailing.

Ivy pressed a finger to the corner of her eye, lifted her chin, and smiled. "Mom and Dad will want photos, so let's make this place spectacular."

Still, she wished their parents could be here.

3

*I*vy walked to the inn's front door with Bev, the bookkeeper she'd hired a few months ago. "You have no idea how relieved I am that you're in charge of the bookkeeping instead of me."

"I hear that a lot," Bev said. "Still, your work wasn't too bad. It hasn't taken me too long to back out your mistakes."

"What you can do in a few hours used to take me several times as long—and many late nights." When she and Bennett returned from their honeymoon, she'd fulfilled her promise to hire extra help so she wouldn't be stretched so thin. To offload tasks like bookkeeping that she wasn't skilled in had made such a difference.

Bev smiled. "Twenty years of focused practice makes it look easy. Sort of like painting, I imagine. I much prefer numbers—I'm a disaster with a paintbrush."

"We're a good match then," Ivy said.

"I'll finish your bookkeeping so you can give it to your accountant to file your tax return. And think about those suggestions we talked about. What you save on taxes, you can use for continued growth."

Ivy opened the front door. "I like the way you think." The

two women hugged before Ivy closed the door. When she turned around, Poppy was walking into the foyer.

"Aunt Ivy, I just got a call from Lea Martin, our guest from Europe. She'd like to arrive early. She's flying from Europe and said it would be easier for her. I told her I would check and call her back."

"I thought we were full. Did you check the reservations?"

Poppy flicked on the computer and peered at the reservation screen. "I saw a cancellation that Shelly entered yesterday. But I didn't know if you wanted to give that to someone on the waitlist."

"Those are people attending the gala." Viola and Meredith were also arriving a few days early. "I think it's safe to book her. Check with Shelly, but we can probably make it work. See if we can shift people around."

Poppy tapped the keyboard. "If I move one couple into another room before they arrive, we can keep Lea Martin in the same room the entire time. She sounds so excited."

Ivy could just imagine. "Let's create a special welcome basket for her room. Include those electrical socket converter plugs we stashed away. I often forget those when I travel." Guests sometimes left items when they lightened their luggage after shopping.

The rear door banged, and they heard Shelly call out. "Where is everyone?"

Poppy answered her, and a few moments later, Shelly appeared, holding Daisy on her hip. "Hey, Ives, are you ready?"

Ivy had no idea what she was talking about. "Ready for what?"

"To go thrift shopping. You didn't forget, did you?"

"I've been working with Bev on the books."

Shelly made a face. "I thought that was her job."

"I still have to answer questions about expenses and review the financial statements Bev creates, but it's getting easier every month." Ivy actually enjoyed the process now. She felt more in control of the business when she could see the inflows and outflows lined up in neat columns.

Shelly slipped off her backpack and gave it to Poppy. "Daisy has just eaten, so she's ready for a nap. We won't be gone very long. If she gets cranky, her favorite toys are in here. I've already set up the playpen in the office, and she can sleep there."

"It's pretty slow right now," Poppy said. "I have one phone call and a few social media posts." She asked Shelly about a guest, Lea Martin, confirming her arrival dates.

This time was the lull in their day—after guests had departed and before others checked in. Today, only one room was turning over, and the new part-time housekeeper, Mary Jane, had already cleaned and changed the room, done the laundry, and left for the day. Between delegating housekeeping and bookkeeping, Ivy had freed up more time to spend with Bennett in the evenings. Their marriage was much better for it.

Shelly started toward the office. "I'll put Daisy down. And thank you for watching her, Poppy."

After Shelly disappeared, the front door creaked open. A young freckle-faced guy barely out of high school poked his head inside. "I have a delivery for Poppy Bay. Is this the right place?"

"That's me," Poppy said.

"Hang on." There was a rustle behind the door, and then the young man pushed the door open wide. "These are for you, then."

He held out a spring bouquet of sunflowers and purple irises wrapped in a bright orange bow.

"Oh, my goodness. It's so colorful." Poppy accepted the arrangement and checked the tiny envelope that was attached.

Ivy's curiosity was piqued. She thanked the delivery guy

and closed the door. After a few moments, she asked, "Who are they from?"

Poppy pocketed the note, her cheeks turning pink with happiness. "This guy I just started dating."

"And does he have a name?"

Poppy shrugged shyly. "Arlo. I've only just met him—well, a few times. I'm seeing him tonight, too. I'll tell you about him later."

Shelly's voice filtered through the hallway as she softly sang a lullaby.

Ivy remembered doing that with her daughters, and it warmed her heart. "It's nice of you to watch Daisy."

Poppy's eyes brightened. "Daisy is so cute, and I love playing with her. I think she understands me."

"Kids learn quickly. She'll be running around here in no time."

Her niece looked thoughtful. "One of my friends from school just had a baby. Sophie, the one who married a year ago. It was so quick."

"That's the way it happens sometimes."

Poppy admired the flowers on the desk and moved them to one side. "Aunt Ivy, how do you know when you've met the right person? Arlo is moving kind of fast, but I don't know if he's Mr. Right or Mr. Right for now. I hear people can change after they marry. How do I know if he will?"

"There aren't any guarantees," Ivy replied, becoming a little worried. "Did he mention getting married already?"

"Sort of. He wants me to move in, but I told him we needed to slow down."

Ivy let out a little sigh of relief. Poppy was smart. "You could be the one who changes, too. You're still in your mid-twenties. Maybe you'll want to do something different, or an opportunity arises. One of your marketing clients could make you an amazing offer."

"I hadn't thought about that," Poppy said slowly. "That could take me to L.A. or New York."

"We'd miss you, but this is the time to explore what you want in life." Ivy paused. "Will we have a chance to meet Arlo soon?"

A smile tugged at Poppy's lips. "I was thinking of running him past you and Bennett or Shelly and Mitch before bringing him home to my parents."

Ivy inclined her head. "Why is that?"

"I met him in L.A. Arlo is a little…older."

"How much older?"

Poppy looked uncomfortable. "He's near your age."

"So, about twenty years older." Poppy was mature for her age, but Ivy had a lot of questions.

She understood why her niece had some trepidation, but Poppy was also a good judge of character. "I assume this is the person you've been on the phone with a lot lately. How did you meet him?"

"When Sunny and I were in L.A., we met them at a party on the Westside."

Ivy inclined her head. "Did you say *them?*"

Suddenly, Poppy's face flushed. "The guy Sunny sort of likes. I thought you knew. That's why I thought you'd be okay with meeting him."

Ivy tried to mask her shock. "Shelly and I would love to meet Arlo."

"Who's Arlo?" Shelly asked as she joined them again.

"The man Poppy is dating. He sent those flowers." Ivy bit her lip. Poppy didn't say Sunny was dating his friend. *Sort of likes.* That wasn't dating. Instantly, she wondered how old he was.

Shelly's eyes glittered with curiosity. "You have to tell me all about him, but Ivy and I have shopping to do. Daisy just drifted off, so the clock is ticking." She tapped her wrist. "Let's go, Ives. We've waited too long to do this as it is."

Ivy and Shelly got into the Jeep, the old vehicle they'd all grown up driving and was still going strong. Shelly liked it because it was roomy enough to hold a lot of baby gear.

Shelly buckled her seatbelt and slid a side-eyed look in Ivy's direction. "You forgot about today, didn't you?"

Ivy sighed. "Okay, I did. But we're doing it now. We have a much larger problem, though." She told Shelly what Poppy said.

"So, she and Sunny are dating a couple of guys." Shelly shrugged. "Those two will date a lot before they settle down. What's more important is making sure we look like a million bucks for this gala."

"Not just a couple of guys. Two men that are my age."

"Oh, yeah?" Shelly shifted and wheeled from the driveway toward town. "Well, Poppy is pretty mature. And I dated tons of older guys."

Ivy shot her a look. "We're also talking about Sunny."

Shelly cracked a grin. "At least this guy won't be copying her midterm paper and nearly getting her expelled from school. What a jerk that last one was."

"This one might be an older jerk. What kind of man in his forties dates a girl who hasn't graduated from college yet?"

Shelly laughed. "A billionaire who wants arm candy? Maybe he'll want to pour money into an old inn."

Ivy swatted her sister. "I'm serious."

"So am I. He could be a tech bro or a crypto king."

"Or a sleazebag with a wife and four kids at home."

"Oh. Well, when you put it like that..." Shelly made a face. "Would it be any better if that was an ex-wife?"

Ivy threw up her hands. "I can't believe we're having this conversation, and you're failing to see the seriousness of it."

"Ivy, people of all different ages fall in love. You haven't even met him. Maybe he's a good guy."

"Sunny hasn't said a word." Ivy pressed a hand to her mouth. "That means she knows I'll disapprove. And just when

I thought she was pulling herself together. What if he side-tracks her? She could fail to graduate this year."

"Come on, what's another year?"

"Seriously, you even have to ask?" Ivy smacked her fore-head in frustration. "More tuition and another year without her working. Honestly, Shells, you have a lot to learn before Daisy starts dating. Ten to one, even Mitch would hit the ceiling. He knows how to figure out people's angles fast."

"Well, he had to, didn't he?" she said softly.

Instantly, Ivy knew she had touched a nerve. "I'm sorry, I didn't mean it that way."

Mitch wasn't proud that he'd served a short prison term for theft when he was young, but he'd learned from his mistake. And he'd been exposed to a lot of characters inside prison.

"I tell him it's a superpower." Shelly shrugged it off. "Actually, I wish someone had warned me about a couple of men I dated. I know we should look out for Sunny and Poppy, but we're up to our eyeballs in work for this gala."

"I'm concerned about Sunny's reaction. You know how she can be."

"That girl runs hot and cold, but she's been pretty good lately."

Ivy told Shelly that Poppy was concerned about taking Arlo to meet her parents. "She asked if we'd meet him. With Mitch and Bennett. I don't know that we have time right now."

Shelly snapped her fingers. "Hey, I've got an idea. I'll tell Poppy that Mitch wants to meet Arlo. Other guys can spot fakes in an instant. If so, problem solved and no time out of our schedule."

The idea was appealing to Ivy. "That's smart. Would you ask Mitch?"

"I'll tell him it's good practice for when Daisy starts dating." Shelly quirked a grin as she pulled into a space in front of Thrifty Threads on a block off Main Street. "Now, we're here. Let the shopping begin."

This was one of Ivy's favorite places to shop. Volunteers ran the store to support animal rescue. The Mabel Baxter Foundation was named after a benefactor who knew the Ericksons. The staff took in dogs, cats, birds, horses, and exotic animals that landed on their doorstep. Relying on their network of pet foster homes and veterinarians, they helped animals find new homes.

A bell on the boutique shop door tinkled as they entered, and a woman with shocking pink hair looked up. It was Gilda, who had been living at the inn since the Ridgetop Fire consumed her home. A Chihuahua lay curled in her lap. Ivy and Shelly greeted them.

"I've just started volunteering here," Gilda said, stroking her diminutive dog. "Pixie's therapist said it would be good for socialization."

"For you or Pixie?" Shelly asked.

Ivy nudged her sister, but Gilda chuckled.

"Both, I guess. We keep to ourselves a little too much."

As a writer, Gilda was usually in her room working on articles for magazines. "This is a perfect place for you two."

"Pixie likes it." Gilda stroked the small dog. "Sometimes I take her to the other side, where they keep the dogs awaiting adoption. She can bark to her heart's content. She's kind of sweet on a miniature Schnauzer. He has a handsome goatee, doesn't he, Pixiekins?"

Pixie looked up and licked Gilda's cheek.

"See? She knows what I'm saying."

"It's good to see you here," Ivy said, aware of Shelly's limited time. "We're looking for evening wear."

"For the gala, I'll bet. Everything we have is right over there." Gilda motioned toward an alcove with a three-way mirror.

Shelly grinned. "Let's do this. *Ciao*, Pixiekins."

Ivy and Shelly sorted through the evening gowns, which were artfully arranged and divided by size.

"There's a lot in your size," Ivy said. Shelly was taller, leaner, and easy to fit. "In mine, not so much."

Shelly had already scooped up several dresses in a rainbow of colors. "What do you think of these?"

"Try them on."

While Shelly slipped into a small dressing room, Ivy continued searching. She held up a bubble-gum pink dress closest to her size. It wasn't her best color, but the lights would be dim. With pink lipstick and the right heels, it might work for one night.

A few minutes later, Shelly emerged from the dressing room in a shimmery, watercolor-blue gown that hugged her in all the right places yet still looked elegant. "I tried the others, but I like this one best. And it will match our ocean theme. What do you think?"

"It's perfect," Ivy replied, admiring the dress. "You don't even have to alter it."

"And the price is right." Shelly grinned as she looked at the price tag. "That was easy. What did you find?"

"Not much in my size." She held up the pink dress. "I'll try this one."

"Well, that's an interesting shade." Shelly lifted an eyebrow. "Wait a minute. I'll see if I can find something else for you." She shuffled through the racks and pulled out a few other choices. "Try these, too."

"Shelly, those would work for you, but look how long they are."

"You can hem them."

"Not the chiffon. That's an art. It's not only the length that needs alteration. I'm short-waisted."

Shelly shoved the dress back. "This one, then."

Ivy wrinkled her nose at it.

"Come on, just try it."

The dress was still a good ten inches too long, but Ivy didn't have time to shop elsewhere. She took the dresses Shelly piled into her arms. "Okay, here goes."

In the dressing room, Ivy tried on dress after dress. Given her petite stature, waistlines fell beneath her natural waist, armholes gaped, and fabric ballooned in the back. Everything was too long or too narrow. While she didn't love the pink dress, it was the closest fit. This event wasn't about her, she told herself. It hardly mattered what she wore.

Ivy swung the door open. "This is the one."

"Are you sure?" Shelly's smile wavered. "It looks like a prom dress."

Admittedly, it did. Ivy felt like a dumpy cupcake in it, but she didn't have time to think about that. "It will look completely different with heels and Mom's pearls."

Gilda appeared behind them. "Well, look at you two glamour girls. Would you like a photo to send to your mother?"

Shelly handed over her phone. Smiling, she wrapped her arm around Ivy.

Gilda took a few photos. "Your mother will love these."

They changed clothes and paid for the dresses. As Gilda was putting plastic over the gowns, another customer arrived. Just then, Ivy caught a glimpse of Pixie streaking past them toward the open door, an emerald-green snakeskin belt trailing behind her.

"Pixie!" Gilda called out. "No, no, sweetie pie."

"I'll grab her," Shelly said, racing after her.

"Has Pixie been borrowing things again?" Ivy asked. The dog was a known kleptomaniac, and she'd been in therapy for a while. They'd learned to keep an eye on small items at the inn, but they knew where to look when something went missing.

Gilda sighed. "My poor baby has regressed a little. That's why her therapist thinks she needs more social stimulation.

Taking care of a dog is so much work. I can't imagine how people manage children."

Smiling, Ivy looped the dresses over her arm. "I'm sure Pixie will be fine."

Shelly lunged onto the sidewalk. "Got her," she cried. Pixie was wriggling beneath her. Just then, a man stooped to help her up.

Ivy stepped outside. "Are you okay?"

"That little dog is fast," the man said, then paused. "Shelly? What are you doing here?"

Instantly, Shelly's cheeks flushed pink. "Oh, my gosh, Grant. Wow, same question." Pixie writhed in her arms like a slippery eel.

Grant reached out to touch Pixie, but the dog growled, and he snapped his hand back. "Is this your guard dog?"

Shelly jerked her away from him. "Oh, she's not mine. But she has good instincts, doesn't she?"

Gilda rushed outside and wrested the belt from Pixie. "You have the best taste, don't you sweetikins?" Cooing to her, Gilda swept Pixie into her arms. "See you all back at the inn."

Ivy watched as Grant laughed, his blue eyes taking in Shelly. "You look good, Shelly. We should grab a drink and catch up. How long has it been?"

Shelly flipped her mussed chestnut hair over her shoulder. "Long enough for me to get married and have a baby."

"No kidding?" He put his hands on his hips and narrowed his eyes. "Are you happy?"

"Ecstatic," Shelly replied. "You're a long way from New York."

"My mother bought a place here a few months ago to be close to friends." He nodded up toward the ridge. "Summer Beach could be much more than a sleepy beach town."

"We've heard that before, but we like it here," Shelly said.

Ivy knew where he meant. The ridgetop estates had incredible ocean views.

"And how is your mother?" Shelly asked.

"As delightful as ever," he said, his tone edged with sarcasm. "She wants me to go to some charity event with her. Sounds like the kind you used to organize for her."

Ivy glanced at Shelly. "Oh? Where is it being held?"

"At an old beach house that someone made into an inn." His eyes glittered. "Supposedly, it has a dark, sordid history. Who knows what went on there? Still, my mother wants to bid on the collector items and support the community."

"Would that be the Seabreeze Inn?" Shelly asked sweetly.

Grant snapped his fingers. "That's it."

Smiling broadly, Shelly said, "That's the one my sister and I run. You'll like it. We have all sorts of sordid affairs there. Just your style." Shelly whipped around and started for the Jeep.

Ivy ducked past him and barely jumped into the vehicle before Shelly shoved the gear into reverse.

"What nerve he has," Shelly said. "Asking me out for a drink as if I would fall at his feet again."

Ivy smoothed the dresses in her lap. "I take it that's one of the guys you never wanted to see again."

Shelly made a face. "You've got that right. What a jerk. His mother is a society queen with a capital Q. Super demanding. At an event she hosted, she once returned dozens of roses for being the wrong shade of red—they didn't match her dress. The event planner lost a lot of money on her. I made sure to get everything in writing with her, including plenty of photographs and documentation. I'm surprised she'd lower herself to Summer Beach standards."

"Maybe she bought that large place next to Carol Reston. Bennett said the buyer was from New York."

"She'll want to glom onto Carol for sure." Shelly shuddered. "We have to be ready to deal with some real characters, Ives. Or this party could get out of hand quickly."

"I'm surprised because Viola and Meredith are such lovely people."

"Don't be so naïve. I hope none of them are staying with us, but the odds aren't in our favor. Not if Grant and Mommie Dearest are here with their crowd."

"I don't care, as long as they bid high. The purpose is to bring the old house up to date." Still, Ivy was concerned about the inn's shabby chic look. Admittedly, some of the rooms were shabbier than chic. "We'd better make some repairs, check the guest list, and be prepared."

Again, Shelly shuddered in her seat. "I don't have a good feeling about this, Ives."

4

*W*hen Bennett walked into Java Beach, he saw Mitch behind the counter. He was wearing a faded Grateful Dead T-shirt. Working among vintage Polynesian posters, beach reggae music, and fishing nets suspended from the ceiling, Mitch brewed the best coffee in Summer Beach. More than that, Java Beach was the place to hear the latest happenings in town.

Mitch ran a hand through his spiky sun-bleached hair. "Want to try my latest beans?"

"Bring 'em on." Bennett watched Mitch's fluid movements around the espresso machine. "I need a strong jolt."

With a flourish, Mitch served up a steaming, dark cup that smelled bold and rich. "Something got you down, man?"

Bennett managed a half-smile. "You know what Wyatt is up to?"

"Yeah. I'm trying to wrap my head around his sudden interest in your gig."

"I suppose he can do what he wants."

"There's talk going around." Mitch leaned on the counter and lowered his voice. "Some say Wyatt wants to use Summer Beach for something bigger."

Bennett frowned, gratefully accepting the cup. "Wouldn't be the first time someone used a position more for personal gain than public service."

Mitch's expression turned thoughtful, and he glanced around before continuing. "There's something else. I overheard a conversation; I don't even like to repeat it. But you should know."

The warmth from the coffee cup in his hands did little to ease the sudden chill Bennett felt. "Go on."

Mitch lowered his voice. "He says he was once involved with your first wife back when she had a college internship in New York City. He even proposed to her, he said."

The revelation hit Bennett with unexpected force. To have that tragedy brought up again would serve no one. Except for Wyatt, in some twisted way. "I don't believe that for a second."

"I'm really sorry, bro. But he had a photo…"

Bennett tried to keep his anger in check. "We all know pictures can be easily altered."

Mitch's eyes grew wide. "Dude, you're right. That's some low stuff he's pulling." Mitch clasped Bennett's hand. "You're rock solid. Don't let Wyatt throw you off course."

Bennett sipped his espresso, which tasted like a bolt of lightning. "Keep me informed, will you?"

"You got it, man. Oh, hey, there's something else. Shelly wants me to meet a guy from L.A. that Poppy is dating. Sort of check him out. I'm not good at this, but she says I'd better learn for Daisy's sake."

"Where are you meeting?"

"Here, on Saturday. Would you mind, uh…" Mitch shifted uncomfortably.

"Let me know what time."

Looking relieved, Mitch grinned. "I owe you one."

Bennett waved it off. "Anything for Poppy. She's a good kid."

Leaving the cafe, Bennett felt the weight of the situation settling onto his shoulders. Wyatt might serve up sensationalism or tell people what they wanted to hear, but his tactics were underhanded. Bennett's commitment to Summer Beach was well-known and long-standing. Surely, residents could see that.

It was still months before residents would vote on who they wanted to lead Summer Beach. A lot could happen before then.

Bennett continued on his weekly walk-about in the village, stopping to visit with shopkeepers to hear their concerns. Reporting to work at his City Hall office was only half his job. The other half was listening to people and being aware of their real needs.

When he strolled past a men's clothing store on Main Street, he paused. In the window was a handsome, under-stated suit.

A casually well-dressed man of about forty came outside. "How's it going, Mr. Mayor?"

"That's what I want to hear from you, Paul. Is business good?"

"Sure is. Lots of spring and summer weddings planned this year." Paul gestured to the dark suit. "That's the latest evening suit I got in. It's popular with those who need a tuxedo but don't want to look like a penguin or a waiter."

Bennett stroked his chin. "Is that suitable for a black-tie event?"

"Are you talking about the fundraiser at the inn?"

"That's the one."

"Perfect. Come in. You can slip one on for size."

Bennett wanted to look his best for Ivy. This benefit was for her, but he didn't want to look out of place among the supporters from the Bay Area. He could get away with a knit shirt and khaki trousers in Summer Beach, even at City Hall. But this was a special event for Ivy.

He followed Paul inside. "Do I have to wear a cummerbund?"

Paul chuckled. "Not unless you want to look like my grandpa or the groom. We have better options."

Bennett relaxed inside the intimate, clubby feeling shop that sported wooden floors, rustic reclaimed wood paneling, and leather chairs. He'd always admired Paul's sense of understated style. He used to work in Chicago but followed the sunshine to Summer Beach a few years ago.

"Try this on." Paul held up a jacket. "It's pure wool with subtle satin lapels and Italian tailoring. Don't let the price tag scare you. It's on sale."

"That's good. It's not something I'd wear often." Bennett had extra funds from the recent sale of an estate next to Carol Reston's home, but he always appreciated a good deal.

Paul brought out a jacket in Bennett's size. "You might be surprised. With the inn getting a facelift, there will probably be many more black-tie events held there. This is a basic part of a professional man's wardrobe. Women love dressing up, and you don't want to disappoint Ivy. This style will last for years."

"That's what I was thinking." He slipped into the jacket Paul held for him and turned around. "What do you think?"

Paul smiled. "Perfect fit. Take a look."

Bennett faced the mirror. Immediately, he stood straighter. "This sure elevates my beach style."

"That will take you anywhere. Add a bow tie for formal events or wear it with a silk tie for a fancy dinner. I like it with an open collar, too. Very cool, very masculine."

"I can see that." He was already imagining where he could take Ivy. After their honeymoon, he'd been thinking about their life together. They'd been talking about a bucket list. She'd mentioned opening night at the opera in San Francisco. He could surprise her with tickets, and maybe they'd stay with Viola.

"What do you think, Mr. Mayor?"

Bennett wouldn't find anything better in Summer Beach, and he wanted to look his best for Ivy. "I'll take it. If you put it aside for me, I'll come back to finish the fitting."

Bennett stepped out into the sunshine, pleased with his decision. He wondered what Ivy planned to wear. Whatever she put on, she'd look beautiful. And he couldn't wait to see what she thought about his new formal suit.

5

*T*hrough the open windows in the foyer, Ivy saw a dark sedan pull in front of the inn. The driver opened the door for a woman. While she collected her purse and got out, he brought her luggage from the trunk and carried it to the front stairs.

Ivy opened the door.

"Is this the Seabreeze Inn?" the young man asked.

When Ivy answered, he brought the suitcases inside and deposited them by the check-in desk. International flights often arrived early in the morning. She imagined this was their guest from Europe.

Ivy welcomed the attractive woman, who looked to be in her early thirties. She was casually dressed in a black jersey knit top and trousers with black loafers. Her soft brown hair had golden highlights, much like Ivy's, although her shoulder-length hair was sleeker and cut in the latest style. Her gold jewelry was simple but looked of good quality.

Her gaze was immediately drawn to a picture in the adjoining parlor of Amelia Erickson. She stared for a moment, then turned to Ivy.

"Hello. I'm Lea Martin." She clutched a large satchel and

gazed around, admiring the foyer. "Thank you for allowing me to arrive early."

Ivy noticed she had only a slight accent. If anything, she sounded almost American. "Did you travel from Berlin?"

"No, from London. I was visiting someone there, so I thought I'd continue with a direct flight to Los Angeles. But going through customs and finding transportation here took longer than I thought it would." Lea stifled a weary yawn. I'm exhausted."

Ivy's heart went out to her. "If you'd like to rest, your room is ready."

"Thank you. I'm so excited to be here." She looked through the door into the ballroom and caught her breath. "The house is stunning."

"Thank you, but it needs work, as you know. We appreciate you coming so far to attend the gala and support our project."

Ivy ached to ask Lea why she was so interested, but she would have another chance after the younger woman could relax and recharge.

Lea touched the banister with reverence. "I have so many questions."

"We have a brochure about the inn, which used to be called Las Brisas del Mar."

"Yes, I read about that. But I really came to learn more about Amelia Erickson and her life here in America. I find it all so intriguing."

Ivy had heard that before. "Amelia was quite an enigma. Since we moved in, we've been trying to piece together her history. She was an amazing woman, but we still have many questions."

Lea brought her gaze back to Ivy and tilted her head. "Maybe I can help you uncover a few new details about her early life."

Ivy detected a change in her new guest's voice. "We always

enjoy learning more about the Ericksons." She paused, uncertain how to reply without drawing the woman into a long conversation. Still, Lea's comment struck her as odd. A little mysterious, even. Quickly, she shook off the feeling. "Shall I show you to your room?"

Lea nodded. "May I have a tour of the home later? I'd love to see where you found the Erickson treasures."

"The lower level is where we have a lot of community meetings." Ivy didn't mention the other locations. "And please let me know if we can provide anything to make your stay with us more comfortable."

Each woman took a suitcase, and Ivy showed Lea to one of their best suites. Ivy thought she seemed quite pleasant. Shelly would be wrong about this guest.

When she opened the door to the suite, Ivy saw Shelly's seasonal floral bouquet, which she had created with early roses and daisies from the garden. On the desk, Poppy had placed a welcome basket filled with snacks, fruit, and bottled water.

Lea's eyes lit with pleasure. "It's just as I imagined it. And you have electrical converters. How thoughtful. I forgot mine."

"The house might be a little dated, but we want you to be as comfortable as possible. Would you like the window open? The fresh air and sound of the ocean might help you rest."

"That would be nice," Lea said, gazing from the window toward the ocean beyond.

Ivy opened the window for her. "You sound like you've spent time a lot of time here in the U.S."

"Not really." Lea smiled. "I watched American television when I was young. That's how I learned conversational English before studying the language in school."

Ivy told her about the wine and tea gathering in the afternoon. After making sure Lea was comfortably settled, she closed the door behind her.

By the time Ivy returned downstairs, Shelly and Poppy

had reappeared with supplies to begin decorating. Shelly carried Daisy in a carrier on her back.

"Our guest from Berlin just arrived," Ivy said.

"Did you find out what brought her all this way?" Shelly asked.

"She was tired from her long journey, but she was in awe of the house, even in its current state."

Poppy placed a bag on the desk. "Even though it needs a lot of work, it's still a beautiful place, Aunt Ivy."

Ivy was still trying to sort out what had struck her as odd about Lea. "She was looking at the house with such reverence, almost as if it had meaning to her."

"Or she was coveting the crystal doorknobs," Shelly said.

Ivy hushed her. "That's a terrible thing to say."

"Why?" Shelly laughed. "It might be true. Do you know what we could get for those?"

Ivy ignored her comment. "And then she said something about helping to uncover details about Amelia Erickson. She might not be here to bid on the necklace or other items. This trip seems more like it's for personal reasons."

"What kind of personal connection could she possibly have?" Poppy asked. "The Ericksons didn't leave any heirs."

Shelly put down another bag of decorations. "She's probably an art fan and read about the collection we found."

That's what Ivy had initially thought. "She has asked for a tour of the house."

"Well, there you have it," Shelly said. "Maybe she's hoping to find more art or jewels stashed away. Be sure to tell her we've already looked everywhere."

Poppy lowered her voice. "Do you really think she might be casing the place?"

"We could have a real jewel thief on our hands," Shelly added in a hoarse whisper. "Don't let her near the vault where we keep the treasure." At that, Daisy squealed and waved her tiny fists with glee.

Putting her hands on her hips, Ivy narrowed her eyes in warning. "That's enough conjecture, and don't start encouraging Daisy. This old house must sparkle for the gala, so we should get started."

"We need to clean first," Poppy said.

Shelly glanced longingly at the decorations. "But we're having so much fun. Doesn't Mary Jane do all the cleaning?"

Ivy rolled up her sleeves. "She's only one person, and you knew we needed to do that first. It's on the list. Come on, with all of us pitching in, it will go much faster. Sunny should be here soon, too. Then we'll have fun decorating. Deal?"

Poppy gave her a high-five. "I'll get cleaning smocks and supplies."

While Ivy would have preferred to hire a cleaning crew, she had to stretch the budget as far as she could. If the necklace fetched a good price at the auction, that would ease the financial burden, but she would still have limited funds to cover so many repairs. A little hard work never hurt, she figured.

Shelly patted her little daughter's hand. "I'll feed Daisy and put her down for a nap."

Ivy kissed the little girl's pink cheeks. "Send your mother back when you're through."

Daisy seemed to promise that with a string of happy sounds.

Lea was the only guest scheduled to check in today. Only two other rooms were occupied. Those couples had gone to the beach, so Ivy hoped to make huge headway this afternoon. She entered the ballroom, her footsteps tapping on the wooden parquet floor.

The first time Ivy saw the old house, the grandeur of this room, even in its dowdy condition, took her breath away. This fundraiser was her chance to restore it to its former glory.

Poppy pushed a cart across the room. "I loaded up with everything we might need. Here's a shirt for you."

Their smocks were an assortment of old work shirts from Bennett and her father that she also used for painting. She slipped one over her blouse and pulled on gloves. "I'll start on the French doors. Why don't you begin on the mantle and fireplace?"

"I love that old piece," Poppy said, running her hand along the mahogany wood and marble. "I'll make it shine."

Ivy turned her attention to the French doors that opened onto the patio. The ocean view beyond was mesmerizing, just as it had been in Amelia's day. She began to clean the windows.

A little while later, Shelly trudged in carrying a ladder. She'd tied a cotton dishtowel around her hair and wore a paper painter's mask around her neck.

"I'll tackle the chandeliers," Shelly said, looking up. "I've been having nightmares about those cobwebs. They're going down right now." She maneuvered the ladder under the first one, its crystals dulled with dust.

Ivy grinned at her sister. "Remember the first time we saw this place?"

"What a mess it was." Shelly shuddered at the memory. "I cried with relief when Flint and Forrest showed up with their kids, and they all went to work."

"I could probably get Reed and Rocky over to help," Poppy offered.

Ivy paused. She was already halfway through the doors. Her brothers and their sons had been a huge help, but they could manage. "I think we'll have this done in a few hours. We had painting and repairs to do then. Cleaning is the easy part. Besides, we might need their help later."

"We've got this." Shelly poked her duster at the cobwebs. "Think of all the calories we're burning. Hey, Poppy, would you turn on the music?"

"Sure." Poppy turned on the music system in the room. "How about some old tunes to get us in the mood?"

"Go for it." Shelly pulled on her mask and whisked a duster across the chandelier. Dust swirled down, and she drew back, squinting against it. "I should have brought goggles, too."

"I have some I use for swimming," Ivy said. "Be right back."

Soon, the melodies of Cole Porter, big band swing, and the Andrews Sisters filled the room, and they sang along as they worked, belting out the words to *Let's Misbehave*, *Anything Goes*, and *The Boogie Woogie Bugle Boy*.

"Woo-hoo, anything goes," Shelly sang, her goggles in place and her voice slightly muffled.

Poppy looked up and grinned. She pressed a finger to her lips and picked up her phone to record Shelly.

Her aunt caught her. "Stop that," Shelly cried, wagging her duster at Poppy, but then she burst out laughing. "Might as well send that to Mitch. That should scare him. He'll never ask me to clean again."

Ivy laughed. "Definitely one of your finer outfits. Maybe you could wear that to the gala."

"Don't tempt me," Shelly said, shaking her duster.

The jazzy music from when this house was in its prime gave rhythm to their work. As time passed, the chandeliers reclaimed their former luster, the mantle glowed with a sheen, and the windows sparkled in the sunlight.

Ivy finished the doors. "Let's misbehave," she sang, dancing across the room to an antique buffet. She swiped a new rag over the surface, cleaning and polishing it with orange oil.

"What a gorgeous piece," she murmured to herself. She enjoyed bringing out the beauty of the handcrafted vintage furniture they had found here. Amelia had exquisite taste and had furnished her home with unique pieces. Even her beach house was fit to entertain royalty.

Ivy felt deep gratitude for the responsibility of caring for this old home. As vexing as it could be with its leaks and flickering lights, she still loved sharing the craftsmanship of a bygone era with visitors and guests.

After opening the drawers, she ran her rag over the finely rendered, dovetailed wood construction. While she was at it, she figured everything needed a good cleaning. She opened a cabinet door on one side and knelt to reach inside.

Ivy's rag snagged on something. "Must be a nail," she muttered. When she tugged on it, the rear panel clattered free. A small, faded red book tumbled to the floor.

"What's that?" Shelly climbed down from the ladder, pulling off her goggles and mask. "I need a break anyway."

Poppy joined them. "We all do. Is this another one of Amelia's treasures?"

"Only if it's stuffed with cash," Shelly said, kneeling beside Ivy.

Ivy sat cross-legged on the parquet floor. "Let's see." The dainty book fit in the palm of her hand, and the leather cover was worn with use.

She opened it and sighed. "Looks like an address book."

"Why would that be hidden?" Shelly asked.

"Who knows?" Ivy replied, turning the brittle pages with care. "We moved this piece from the library to make room for another desk and printer, remember?"

Poppy peered over her shoulder at the feathery script. "Look at all those addresses. Germany, Austria, Switzerland, Paris. It must have been Amelia's. Who else would have tucked it away?"

"Maybe it was her husband's," Ivy replied thoughtfully. "Or it might have belonged to one of her guests from the attic."

Each page was a careful collection of mostly European addresses. Ivy leaned in, her finger hovering over an entry as if touching it might whisk her back in time.

She turned another page and sighed. "Look at this one.

Mallorca." She thought of the woman she and Bennett had met in the train station who invited them onto her brother's boat. "Maybe this was Raquel's grandfather."

She grew quiet, thinking about how much Amelia must have treasured these links to their past in Europe. But why hide it?

"Maybe when Amelia turned this house into a physical therapy and recovery center for injured service members, she tucked away things of value." Ivy looked at the entries again. "Or, these names might have implicated her or other people."

"In what?" Poppy asked.

"Maybe a huge art heist," Shelly said, shaking dust from her goggles.

Ivy clicked her tongue and frowned. "That wasn't a heist —she was sheltering those works. That was confirmed." She hesitated. "Maybe these were some of her connections for that endeavor."

"Or family and friends," Poppy ventured. "She would have wanted to keep those safe, especially during the war."

"But she had no family left," Ivy said sadly. Still, this small address book was a portal into the past, each address a chapter of Amelia's storied life. "This is amazing. All these people knew her."

Shelly brushed a cobweb from her hair and cringed. "But they're all long gone."

Ivy considered that. "Megan might want to track down people who knew them. They might have heard stories about the Ericksons. Like the people we met on Mallorca."

As Ivy passed the small book around, the sense of connection to the inn's history was palpable. They were not just preparing for another event; they were custodians of a legacy, ensuring that the stories and spirits of those who had danced and dined in this ballroom would live on.

Poppy handed the address book back to her. "We should keep that safe."

"Maybe we can display it at the gala," Ivy said. Just then, a thought struck her. "We should keep a modern history of the inn. Someday our grandchildren might be asking about all this, or who visited or was married here."

"I could start a daily journal," Poppy said.

Shelly nudged Ivy. "Think of all we could include. Like the time you pulled Rowan Zachary from the pool. Drunk actor escapades have to go in there."

Ivy smiled and brushed a lock of hair from her forehead. Yet, she couldn't shake the feeling that these names had special meaning to Amelia.

Could one of these entries open a window to her past?

*a*fter thoroughly cleaning the ballroom, Ivy showered and changed into a spring-feeling lavender blouse and floral skirt to prepare for the evening wine and tea reception in the music room. She expected their new guest, Lea, would join them unless she was still sleeping off her jet lag.

Ivy was removing the covering from the appetizers when she heard footsteps behind her.

"Hey, Mom." Sunny breezed in wearing a T-shirt and jean shorts. Her hair looked windblown and her nose and cheeks were slightly sunburned. "I'm famished. Can I have some of those?"

"These are for guests. You know where the kitchen is." She paused. "It's near the ballroom, but it seems you had trouble finding that this afternoon."

Sunny clapped a hand over her mouth. "Oh, the cleaning. I completely forgot."

"You don't look like you've been studying either."

"I took a break and went out with some friends."

"Here?"

"No, up in L.A. In Venice Beach. It's pretty cool."

"What about that midterm paper you have due?"

Sunny heaved a sigh. "I'll get around to it."

"You haven't started?" When her daughter shook her head, Ivy pursed her lips. "If I'd known that, I wouldn't have asked you to help us. Make yourself a snack and start working on the paper. I'll make dinner after the welcome reception."

A guilty look washed over Sunny's face. "I'm going out again."

"To work on your paper?"

Sunny looked away.

"Who are these friends taking you away from your midterm paper?" Sunny only shrugged, and Ivy put a hand on her hip. "Setting up for the reception was supposed to be one of your jobs here. All of us are happy to pitch in when you need to study, but don't ruin your grades. You're so close to graduation. I thought after last semester, you were back on track."

"I will be." Sunny blew out an exasperated breath. "You don't get it, Mom. I need a life, too."

Ivy waited, but Sunny didn't divulge anything else. "Is this about someone you're dating?"

Sunny let out a huff. "We're just hanging out, okay?"

"Honey, your main objective is to finish school." If Ivy could send her adult daughter to her room and ground her, she would. "If you don't, you'll have to figure out how to pay for your tuition."

Sunny's mouth dropped open. "You're joking."

"I certainly am not. I worked my way through school. If you're going to abuse my generosity, then you can learn what it's like to earn your way. You'll be doing that soon enough, anyway. Now, if you don't want to do that, I suggest you stay in tonight and start working on your midterm paper."

Sunny crossed her arms. "I wish Dad were still here. He let me do whatever I wanted."

Ivy bit back a comment. That was the root of their problems. Whatever rules Ivy had instituted, Jeremy ignored. He wanted to be adored, so he let the girls do whatever they pleased. Misty managed to develop a keen sense of responsibility, but Sunny was still working on that.

"What do you think your father would have done in this situation? About your midterm, I mean."

Sunny glanced nervously at the antique clock ticking on the mantle. "I don't know. Paid a tutor, I guess."

"Do you think you need a tutor for this project?"

Sunny looked away and shook her head. "No. I can do it."

Ivy tucked a wayward strand of hair behind Sunny's ear. "You're so close to finishing school, sweetheart. You're an adult now, so you need to consider your priorities. Don't be concerned about pleasing your friends. True friends will understand and support you in your efforts. Think about what you're doing. That's all I ask."

Sunny's cheeks flushed. "I won't be out late. I can start working on the project when I get back."

Ivy hoped she would. Then, she thought about the conversation she'd had with Poppy. Was this about the man Sunny liked? Ivy wondered if he was also a lot older than her daughter.

A young girl appeared in the doorway. She appeared a little anxious and awkward, biting her lower lip. "Excuse me, Poppy told me to come back here. I'm supposed to play the piano tonight." She introduced herself as Abby. "My teacher, Mrs. Green, said I can practice during your party."

Ivy smiled and gestured toward the piano. "I'm so glad you're here. We love having her students. Make yourself comfortable."

Twisting her hands, Abby said shyly, "My mom is waiting in the car. Do you think she could come in, too? I've never played such a nice a piano, and I want her to see it, but Mrs. Green said I need to be professional." She chewed a fingernail, smearing her pink lipstick as she did.

"Of course." Ivy smiled and motioned to the girl's chin. "How old are you, Abby?"

"Twelve." The young girl wiped her chin with the edge of her sleeve. "Everyone says I'm tall for my age."

With her hair and makeup done and wearing what was probably her best dress, Abby looked older, but her youth showed. Ivy understood her nervousness. "My daughter Sunny will bring you a glass of lemonade and set up a tip jar for you." She lowered her voice. "There are tissues beside the piano. You don't need to wear lipstick here if you don't want to."

Smiling self-consciously, Abby looked relieved and went to get her mother.

Turning to Sunny, Ivy added, "The water and lemonade pitchers are in the kitchen."

Sunny shot her another look of annoyance, but Ivy held firm. "You need to change fast and finish setting up."

Again, Sunny blushed but hurried out, mumbling as she went.

Quickly, Ivy folded the napkins and arranged the silverware that Amelia had once used.

Just a few months ago, Ivy had been so proud of Sunny and her new-found maturity. What on earth had happened to her? Somehow, she had to help Sunny regain that. Maybe treating her like an adult and letting her solve her own problems would work again. But she hated to see Sunny fail a class and not graduate.

Just then, Shelly opened a screen door to the veranda and motioned to her. "Mom is on the phone and wants to talk to you. Mitch will be here soon to pick us up. He's bringing freshly baked cookies for guests, too."

Abby began playing the piano softly, and Ivy gave her a thumbs-up. She stepped outside, where Shelly was sitting with Daisy. Her parents were in port, and she didn't want to miss them before they set sail again. Calling from open seas was expensive, and they reserved that for emergencies. Sunny could finish setting up, especially since she planned to go out.

Ivy took the phone. "Hi, Mom. Having a good time out there?"

"Simply wonderful," Carlotta replied. "We met old friends for dinner last night. The Carringtons. They used to live across the street when you were in elementary school. I'll send photos later."

"I'd love to see them." Ivy could hear the subtle jingle of the silver bangles her mother often wore. She closed her eyes, enjoying the sound and her mother's voice.

"Are you still there, *mija*? Sometimes the phone connection drops, so we should speak fast."

"I'm here, Mom." Ivy looked forward to her parents' emails and texts. She liked following their grand adventure and was so proud of them for seizing the chance.

"Shelly has been telling me all about your plans for the gala. How I wish we could be there. I'd love to meet Viola and Meredith."

"I'm sure you will when you return. We could take a trip to San Francisco. You'd love Viola's home."

"Oh, just a moment, tell Shelly her photo just made it to me. The connection is quite slow. Now, let me open it. I can't wait to see what you girls bought."

Ivy turned to Shelly. "What did you send her?"

"The photo that Gilda took at Thrifty Threads."

"Oh, my goodness, just look at you, Ivy!" Carlotta chuckled. "You had me going there. Now, really. What are you wearing to the gala? Something chic, I'm sure."

Ivy's mouth dropped open, and she turned back to her sister.

Shelly cringed and held up her hands. "I tried to tell you."

"That's what I'm wearing, Mom. It's the only thing I could find that doesn't need extensive alterations. There's no time for that. We have an entire house to clean and decorate, guests to welcome, and a long to-do list." She shot another look at her sister. "Shelly is lucky; she can fit into anything."

Her mother's voice softened with concern. "But surely you have something other than a frilly pink prom dress in your closet. Why, you used to dress beautifully in Boston when you and Jeremy went out. Don't you have any of those dresses?"

"That was years ago. They were too small and dated, so I gave them away before I left Boston." After her husband's death, Ivy had been consumed with grief and overwhelmed with the financial shambles he'd left in his wake.

She lifted her chin and tried to make light of the situation. "With heels and pearls, the dress will look completely different."

Shelly looked doubtful.

Ivy felt like she was trying to convince herself and her mother. She clutched the phone as words tumbled from her lips. "Anyway, Viola and her guests are the stars of the evening. We'll dim the lights. This will only be a few hours. No one will care how I look."

Carlotta let out a small sigh. "I'm sorry, *mija*. I didn't mean to find fault with you. I trust your judgment, but I thought you might like to wear something special for the gala. It is an important event."

That was true. The inn's future depended on the outcome of the gala auction. Ivy pinched the bridge of her nose. "A dress I might wear only once is not in my budget."

"I'd be happy to call a shop there and give them my credit card," Carlotta said, a note of hope in her voice. "Even a simple, floor-length black skirt with a silk blouse and pearls would be elegant and understated."

"At the very least, a skirt would still have to be hemmed." Ivy pressed her fingers to her throbbing temple. "They're all way too long on me. I appreciate the advice, but I'm afraid I live in sundresses and jeans." Maybe she had made a mistake in buying that dreadful dress. But it was too late now.

From the corner of her eye, she saw a woman who looked like Abby enter the music room, followed by two of their guests. She told her mother goodbye before handing the phone back to her sister.

Shelly's face crumpled with sympathy. "I'm sorry I sent that photo, Ives. Mom wanted to know what we planned to wear. I wasn't thinking."

"It will be fine." Ivy clasped Shelly's hand. "But when I'm through with that dress, I promise I'll donate it back to Thrifty Threads."

Shelly nodded toward the music room. "There's Sunny. I think she's looking for you. Is that other woman our guest from Europe?"

"No, that's the mother of our student pianist. We might not see Lea Martin until tomorrow morning. She had a long flight."

Ivy relieved Sunny of her duties, although Sunny stayed to help. At least her daughter had thrown a sundress over her shorts and brushed her hair. She had also poured wine for their guests. Abby's mother had opted for lemonade. A few minutes later, Mitch arrived with freshly baked chocolate chip cookies, which Sunny passed around.

Ivy stayed and chatted for a while, giving their guests restaurant recommendations. She also answered questions about the special spa and culinary weeks they hosted at the inn during the winter off-season. Those had been gaining in popularity and augmented their income.

As Ivy visited with guests, she listened to Abby play. Then, she approached the young girl's mother and introduced herself.

"Thank you for having her," the other woman said. "I'm Marsha, and I can't tell you how much this means to her. It's her first public performance, other than recitals."

"Your daughter is quite talented," Ivy said. "She's handling herself very well."

"Once she starts playing, she gets carried away by the music. I had no idea she would pick up the piano so fast, but Mrs. Green had faith in her. She lets her practice after school, sometimes for hours."

"She can come here anytime, too. We welcome students in the school's music program. I love to hear the kids playing after school and on the weekends."

They had a steady stream of young pianists, violinists, and singers. One teenager played the flute, and another brought a cello. Ivy liked to think that Amelia would have approved.

"Say, I have an idea," Ivy said. "We're having a large fundraiser here to raise money for historical preservation. It would be nice to feature our young musicians. Do you think Abby would like to play one piece?"

Marsha broke into a smile. "Wow, that would be amazing. I'll see if she's up to it. She's a little shy."

Ivy glanced at Abby, who was lost in her music. "It seems once she starts playing, she's fine."

Marsha nodded with pride. "I'll talk to her."

"And I'll speak to Mrs. Green at the school."

Feeling confident about such an addition to the event, Ivy excused herself. Soon, the other guests left for their dinner plans in town.

"Hey, Mom." Sunny approached her with her head dipped. "Do you mind if I take off now?"

Ivy wasn't pleased, but Sunny would do what she wanted. "Go ahead. Be home early like you promised."

"And I'll start my paper, honest I will." Sunny was fidgeting, twirling a strand of her wavy strawberry blond hair. She seemed eager to flee.

Ivy remembered what it was like to be young and crazy about someone. "Okay, but let's talk later tomorrow. I want to hear all about your evening." And whoever was jeopardizing her daughter's schoolwork.

*a*rthur opened the door to Antique Times for Ivy and Shelly, who dashed in from the morning shower. "Welcome, and come in out of the rain. You may stash your brolly in the corner."

Ivy brushed raindrops from the shoulders of her sky-blue dress. The linen fabric was wrinkly and washable linen, so it was fine. She had been holding the umbrella over Daisy.

Shelly wore a blouse with a flowing skirt and carried Daisy on her hip. The little girl was already fascinated with the unusual pieces in the shop.

"What's a brolly?" Shelly asked, looking perplexed. "Surely you don't mean Daisy."

Ivy and Arthur laughed. Originally from England, he often used different words than they did. "He means your umbrella. As the saying goes, we're divided by a common language."

"Right, then." Arthur chuckled and ran a hand over his bald head. "You're interested in the old captain's wheel. There she is."

"If you can lend it to us for the gala, we'd appreciate it."

Ivy loved visiting this shop on Main Street. She followed him to the window.

"This is a sweet old relic," Arthur said, touching the vintage wooden wheel. "Nan has been after me to get rid of this for some time. It has quite a history that we can share."

Shelly eyed the antique wheel. "Maybe we'll find a buyer for you."

Arthur's eyes gleamed behind his wire-rim glasses. "I'm happy to lend it to you for decorations for the gala, but do you think you might have a place for it in your auction? As a contribution to the cause."

"That's very generous of you," Ivy replied, pleasantly surprised. "Are you sure you want to part with it?"

Arthur chuckled. "That's what we do here. Inventory turnover keeps us in business. We can use the donation write-off for tax purposes; frankly, we need the room for fresh merchandise. And it's for a good cause, isn't it?"

"The best," Shelly said, grinning. "Let's load it into the Jeep."

Arthur held up a hand. "It's heavy and cumbersome. I can have it delivered later. Are others in Summer Beach donating items to the auction?"

Ivy nodded. "Our next stop is Carol Reston's home. She offered an autographed sheet of music from one of her hit songs. We'll have it framed."

"That should bring in a tidy sum," Arthur said, nodding. "We have some high-profile clients I could ask as well."

The offer meant a lot to Ivy, and she touched her heart with gratitude. "I wouldn't want to trouble you, but we can use all the help we can get."

There was once a time when Ivy was reluctant to ask for help or favors. But after living in Summer Beach, she'd learned how much neighbors looked after and helped each other here. Maybe it was because the community was small, and word of those in need traveled fast. She was happy to do her part whenever she could. Living here changed a person; she'd experienced it, and she'd witnessed the transformations as well.

Like Mitch. The community had faith in him now.

She reached for Shelly's hand. "We appreciate this, Arthur. We're looking forward to seeing you and Nan at the event."

"We wouldn't dream of missing it."

The rain had let up, so Ivy tucked the umbrella under her arms and held the door for Shelly and Daisy.

As Shelly buckled Daisy into her car seat, she looked up at Ivy. "Have you thought about what we could donate to the auction?"

"Like something that belonged to the Ericksons?"

"Sure. Viola is donating the necklace and a tea set."

"What we've found is going into the historical collection for the community area." They were already using the lower level for events.

Shelly slid into the driver's seat and started the Jeep. "Don't you wish we'd kept at least one of the paintings we found? Those were worth a fortune."

Even one of the small ones would have bailed them out of the financial abyss long ago. But wishing didn't make it right.

"The families were thrilled to have their property returned. None of that was ours to keep." Ivy stared from the window, an idea forming in her mind.

Daisy squealed from the backseat, and Shelly turned on some music. "She likes listening to tunes in the car, especially pop music. Don't you, sweetie pie?"

Ivy smiled, remembering when she did that with her girls. Soft music put them to sleep, but Ivy knew Carol wanted to see Daisy.

Shelly turned onto the road that led to the ridgetop. The rain stopped as she drove, so she opened the windows. The path climbed high above the coastline, and the sound of the waves receded as they drove. In the backseat, Daisy's contented claps and hums provided a sweet background chorus that entertained Ivy and Shelly.

"She's expressive," Shelly said, brushing her hair from her face.

"Can't imagine where she gets that from," Ivy added with a wink. The open windows brought the fresh scent of moist earth after the rain on the sea breezes.

Ivy watched the scenery blur past while she returned to her thoughts. Sunshine peaked through morning clouds over the drenched landscape. Each bend in the road brought inspiration until, finally, the inn below came into view. From above, it looked like a seaside oasis.

She tried to imagine what Summer Beach must have looked like to Amelia and Gustav before they built their home here. There hadn't been much here, but she'd had the foresight to build a grand home on the sea and even help lay out parts of the town—another fact that Megan had discovered in her research.

With her mind cleared and focused, she turned to Shelly.

"I have an idea," she began. "Just picture Amelia Erickson standing on the front steps of Las Brisas del Mar, gazing across the sands and out to sea, determined to right wrongs and create a parcel of paradise here. Can you see her?"

Shelly nodded, playing along. "She was formidable, that's for sure."

Ivy's gaze drifted to the backseat, where Daisy gurgled happily. "I want to capture that feeling. Amelia, in her element, but I want to do it in a way that's, well, transcendent. Not just Amelia as we saw her in photographs and in that silent film clip, but as the essence of what she stood for and the difference she made in people's lives—then, and for generations."

Shelly nodded thoughtfully. "Like Nick, our Christmas guest. She threw pebbles that rippled far and wide."

"I could auction a painting." The idea took root in Ivy's mind, growing insistently. She envisioned Amelia Erickson, not as the sepia-toned photograph in the lobby of the Seabreeze Inn, but alive and in color, her presence as formidable on canvas as it had been in life.

Shelly arched an eyebrow in doubt. "But how could you have that finished for the gala?"

"I couldn't, but I think I can have a sketch ready. I could auction that with a promise for a painting. Sort of like a commissioned work, but by auction."

"Why not just put one of your seascapes up for auction?"

"I'm happy to do that," Ivy said, drawing a hand across her forehead. "I can't explain it, but I feel I have to do this—to show her strength and the facets of her personality."

"What we know of her, that is."

"We're discovering more and more." Ivy sketched an image in the air as she spoke. "The Amelia who dared to smuggle great art from Europe during the war for safekeeping. The woman who provided passage and new lives to people displaced. The woman who opened her home to the wounded yet built a fortress beneath her to alleviate her fears. The public figure and the private dreamer. I want to paint her on the steps, the wind in her hair, the inn behind her, and the ocean before her. In her eyes, a reflection of what she loved."

Ivy could almost see the brushstrokes that would bring Amelia to life.

"It sounds beautiful, Ives. It's like you're bringing her back for a standing ovation." Shelly glanced in the rearview mirror, grinning at Daisy before returning her eyes to the road.

Ivy's heart swelled at the thought. "Amelia gave so much of herself to others—and us. This painting will be my way of saying thank you. Of keeping her legacy alive and inspiring others to take up her torch."

Shelly heaved a sigh. "It seems cruel that a woman like that was robbed of her fabulous memories later in life."

Ivy recalled the tumultuous time of history Amelia lived through and what she fought against. "Maybe she didn't mind forgetting some things. At any rate, I feel like I must pay tribute to her, using whatever skill I can muster."

Shelly shot her a lop-sided grin. "I think you should do it. Be sure to tell Viola and Meredith."

That felt right, too, Ivy thought. But she would wait until they arrived. Until then, she wanted to let her artistic vision settle in her heart and flow onto paper.

Shelly pulled to the gated entry of the estate where Carol and her husband Hal lived. She reached out and pressed the call box button. "It's Ivy and Shelly."

The speaker crackled. "Come right in." The gates swung open.

The grand estate spread out before them, bringing back memories for Ivy. "Remember when we escaped up here from the tsunami threat?"

Shelly nodded as she parked near the entrance. "That was kind of Carol and Hal to open their doors to so many folks in need. And Mitch had a great time cooking for the crowd in their fancy kitchen."

That was another treasured memory they shared. "We've had a good time here in Summer Beach, haven't we, Shells?"

"You bet. And we met a couple of great guys."

At that, Daisy giggled with joy and waved her tiny hands.

"I knew you'd be happy about that," Shelly said, laughing. "You can thank me when you're old enough to understand."

"Don't count on it." Ivy smiled and thought about Sunny. "How old were we when we finally realized how fantastic our parents were?"

Shelly got out and unlatched Daisy from her car seat, smoothing her wispy blond hair. "I know what you're thinking. Sunny will come around again. She's just testing her wings."

Just then, the front door opened, and Carol stepped out to greet them. She was a petite powerhouse with sassy henna-red hair. She wore white jeans and glittery sneakers with what looked like a vintage Pucci blouse—a colorful, bold work of art itself.

"It's so good to see you two," Carol said, throwing her arms wide. "Oh, make that three. Hello, little one. May I hold her?"

Daisy brightened at Carol's voice and reached for her brightly colored blouse. Shelly passed her daughter to Carol, and they made their way inside.

Carol nodded toward a bag Miranda, her housekeeper, was organizing for her on a bench by the door. "The sheet music with lyrics is in there, but we also assembled a collection of other items you can auction. I found some lyrics I'd jotted down that people might get a kick out of. Hal wrote up a little story about each item."

Through the expansive glass windows and doors, the view of Summer Beach and the ocean beyond was spread out before them like one of Ivy's seascapes.

As if reading her mind, Carol said, "Hal and I were at a music festival and had dinner in Sausalito one night. Imagine my surprise when I saw your paintings of that view in a gallery."

A tall, good-looking man with electric blue-framed glasses appeared behind them. Hal greeted them with enthusiasm. "The gallery owner was excited to see us, but we were more excited to see your work there. Our friends fell in love with it and bought one of your pieces."

Ivy was surprised. "What a small world. And thank you for showing it to them."

"We didn't," Carol said. "They were the ones who saw it first."

"We want to hear all about the gala," Hal said.

They gathered in the kitchen to talk about it. Their resident chef, Raul, who was from Argentina, was reviewing the menu for the week. Mitch had cooked with him during the natural disaster. Raul started a fresh pot of coffee for them and offered them homemade pastries.

Carol had agreed to sing, and Ivy was thrilled. Viola and Meredith loved her music.

"You don't have much more time," Carol said. "Is there anything you need help with? I can volunteer Hal."

Her husband laughed. "I'm surprisingly handy with tools, but don't let that get around. That's the farm boy in me."

"We've already scrubbed our fingers to the bone," Shelly said. "The old inn is sparkling. Well, the chandeliers are anyway, thanks to yours truly."

"But we appreciate the offer." Ivy almost had to pinch herself. Here she was, having coffee and chatting with Carol Reston, a well-known Grammy Award winning singer who was also friendly and down to earth. The couple had retreated to Summer Beach to live how they wanted away from the limelight. Bennett had known them as neighbors for years.

They talked about the event for a bit longer, and then Ivy's phone buzzed with a text message.

"Who needs us?" Shelly asked.

"It's Poppy. Sounds like she needs us."

"I'm sure you have a thousand things to do," Carol said, handing Daisy back to her mother. "But I'm so happy you brought Daisy to see me." She tapped Daisy's nose. "I think we're going to be good friends, little one. I'll teach you how to sing."

Daisy cooed her approval and gave her a toothless grin.

Hal smiled fondly at his wife. "She's always had a soft spot for kids."

A few minutes later, Ivy and Shelly finished saying their goodbyes. As they got into the old Jeep, Daisy waved, too.

"We need to go straight back to the inn," Ivy said, buckling her seatbelt.

Shelly turned the key in the ignition. "What's up? You had a strange look when that text came in."

"It's Lea Martin."

"The new guest? Is she giving Poppy grief?"

"Something happened. Poppy said she's asking a lot of questions, and she's a little uncomfortable answering them."

Shelly steered toward the gate, which slid open for them. "Like what?"

"She didn't say. But for Poppy to reach out, that's something."

Shelly looked at her with understanding and turned onto the street. "We'll be there as fast as we can."

Ivy wondered what had troubled Poppy. Her niece had a fairly well-tuned sense about guests.

She glanced at Shelly. "Maybe we should count those crystal doorknobs after all."

8

"*W*here is Lea?" Ivy asked as soon as she returned. Poppy's text about Lea had seemed urgent, so she and Shelly drove straight back from Carol Reston's home.

"I sent her for a walk on the beach to calm down," Poppy said, seeming on edge. "I think you need to talk to her."

"Did you count the doorknobs?" Shelly asked, shifting Daisy onto her hip. The little girl was getting cranky.

Ivy silenced them both with a stern look.

Poppy looked confused. "I don't know what you're talking about."

"Sorry, inside joke," Shelly said, fishing a rattle from her shoulder bag for Daisy.

Poppy clasped her hands. "Lea was asking questions about —" When another guest strolled into the foyer, she stopped speaking.

"Take your time." Ivy touched Poppy's hand and was surprised to find her trembling. "Lea told me she knew something about Amelia Erickson. Did she say what it was?"

"No, it wasn't that." Poppy cast an unsettled look upstairs.

"We should go up there and find out what happened, but I don't want to go alone."

Ivy traded a look with Shelly. "Did something happen to Lea up there?"

"I should let her tell you." Poppy's eyes were wide. "I couldn't quite make it out, except that…" She nodded toward the other guest. "I offered to call a doctor for her."

"Was she ill or feeling faint?" Ivy rubbed Poppy's hands.

"More like hysterical," Poppy whispered. "That's why she went to the beach—to let the ocean air calm her nerves."

As soon as the other guest left, Poppy clutched Ivy's hand. "She said she saw something in her room."

"Something like…" Ivy was still perplexed. "A rat?"

Still speaking in a hushed tone, Poppy continued, "An apparition."

"Oh, here we go," Shelly said. "I'll put Daisy in her playpen, then we're going up there."

"Wait," Ivy said, grabbing Shelly's arm. "Poppy, was it friendly, or—"

"Do we need an exorcist?" Shelly finished.

Ivy whipped around to face her sister. "Would you behave? This is serious. What if there's an unfriendly…thing…"

"You can say it," Shelly said. "Boo!"

"Stop it." Ivy stamped her foot and gestured to Poppy. "Whatever it was, it was upsetting to Lea. Poppy, you stay here, I'll talk to Lea, and Shelly, you take the master key and see if you find anything."

Shelly gave a nervous laugh. "Look, I'm not afraid to say what it is, but I'm not crazy enough to go up there alone."

Ivy shook her head. "We're going to have an inn full of people soon, and I will not have something like *The Shining* going on here. Let's go up there together and…"

Shelly raised her eyebrows. "What? Reason with—"

"Yes." Ivy straightened her shoulders. "We haven't come this far to be intimidated by…whatever," she added in a hoarse whisper. If guests heard this conversation, it would spread like wildfire. People might check out, and she wouldn't blame them.

"Lea was probably imagining something," Ivy said. "A long flight, lack of sleep, different time zones, strange food."

Shelly laughed. "That airline food will make you see some spooky stuff."

Exasperated, Ivy snatched the master key, placed her foot on the first step, and turned around. "Well? Who's coming with me?"

"Oh, alright." Shelly grabbed Poppy's hand. "Let's go. There's power in numbers. Daisy, you, too." The little girl shook the rattle with a vehemence. "That's right, Daisy-do. You're fearless."

Poppy shuddered. "I keep thinking about that Amityville movie you made me watch as a kid."

Shelly gave her an apologetic look. "I'm sorry. I had no idea that would keep you up all night."

Trying to appear nonchalant, they crept upstairs, the steps creaking as they climbed. In the lead, Ivy craned her neck to see the floor as they rose to the second story. She sniffed the air for curious scents.

"Nothing yet." Ivy wasn't sure what she was looking for, but whatever it was, it wasn't of this world. Lea was spooked. She would likely want to change rooms at the very least.

Behind her, Shelly whispered, "What will you do when we get there?"

"I'm no expert at this." Ivy pressed a hand to her pounding heart. "I figure we'll have a chat, that's what."

Shelly burst out laughing. "You're going to reason with—"

"Well, what do you suggest?" Ivy cleared the last step. Squaring her shoulders, she turned toward Lea's room.

She slipped the key in the door and opened it. The room was dim. She flicked on the light.

The suite looked as if Lea had just left. The bedcovers

were tossed aside, and a book lay open on the floor. Ivy walked to the bed and turned around, following what would have been her line of sight.

Shelly gingerly stepped inside. "What do you see, Sherlock?"

"Maybe she was reading. Or taking a nap." Ivy peered across the room. "Could have been a shadow in that corner, or maybe that one? Or there, by the bathroom?"

Poppy crossed the room and peeked inside the adjoining bath. "I don't see anything." She checked the windows. "They're all closed."

Shelly shivered and tightened her grip on Daisy, who simply stared. "You don't think they were going to hang out and wait for us, do you?"

"Lea sensed something." Ivy didn't like to admit it, but she'd also felt odd sensations in the past. Not in this suite but in the primary bedroom, which had been Amelia's. Cold spots, shadows, but mostly the unsettling sense that she was not alone.

These feelings might have been mere products of her imagination. If Ivy were to admit possibilities as spirits and ghosts existed, that would open to the door even more questions. She didn't have the time or strength for that.

She turned to Shelly. "You're the one who believes in all this. What do you feel?"

"Actually, nothing. I'm pretty disappointed."

"At least there aren't any rattling chains," Poppy said. "But it seems tense in here. I think we should move Lea."

Ivy considered this. "That's one solution. Have we ever had a complaint about this room?"

The others shook their heads. "I suppose a spirit could wander around," Shelly offered.

Ivy stretched out her hands. "Let's have a chat with her."

Poppy's eyes widened. "You think it's Amelia?"

"What can it hurt? Maybe she's wondering what's going

on." She didn't want to share the sensations she had felt before. They all clasped hands, and Ivy drew a deep breath.

"Hello, Mrs. Erickson? I want to tell you about the gala we're having to restore Las Brisas del Mar," Ivy began, feeling a little silly. She talked about the repairs they needed to make and the friends coming to visit. "Maybe you know Viola from San Francisco. And you should hear about the menu. Everything will be fabulous, served on your fine china, of course. Not in league with your parties, but everyone will surely enjoy themselves. " As Ivy spoke, a sense of peace descended around her.

They were quiet for a moment, and then Poppy said, "I think that did it."

Ivy smiled. "Everyone likes to be informed. Now, I have to find Lea, and I hope she hasn't booked a flight home. Poppy, would you help her move? And Shelly, find another room for her. I'll bring her back."

As Ivy closed the door, a movement caught her eye. The sheer fabric covering the windows swayed slightly.

"And Poppy, check the house fan."

"It's not on," Poppy said, holding her hand to a vent. "We haven't turned it on yet. The nights are still a little cool, and it's not that warm in the daytime yet."

Ivy glanced back at the room, now at a loss for words. Was that a sweep of appreciation or a whisper of goodbye? At any rate, it wouldn't hurt to move Lea.

She walked outside and spotted Lea near the water's edge. She started toward her.

"Hello," Ivy called out, her sneakers sinking in the soft sand near the house.

Lea turned, the wind whipping her hair. She raised a hand.

When Ivy reached the wet sand, the shoreline grew firmer underfoot, and she lengthened her stride toward Lea. "Hello, I heard you had a fright."

"Your niece must have told you." Lea brushed a hand over her hair. "She's lovely, by the way. Now, I'm not so sure what happened, but it seemed so real at the time. It was those sheer curtains, and then this…" She paused, and a shudder coursed through her.

"Old houses have a lot of creaks," Ivy said quickly. "Have you ever lived in one before?"

She wasn't sure whether to minimize the incident or discuss what had happened. There wasn't much Ivy could do other than hope it wouldn't happen again.

"This might sound funny, but often I feel my grandmother's presence," Lea said. "I think there are times when only a thin line separates us, or maybe those are echoes of the past that we pick up on, like a radio frequency."

"That's a sweet thought," Ivy said, considering the idea. That might explain a lot, but who knew? "It might be the wishes of our hearts, too."

"That could be. I wish my grandmother were still here with me. I have so many questions I wished I'd asked her, but I was only a little girl." Lea stuffed her hands into the pockets of her denims. "It might sound odd, but I felt like I wasn't alone, and then the curtains… I didn't expect that here, so I got scared. But maybe here, of all places, I should have been prepared for it."

Ivy wasn't sure what Lea meant by that. Instead of asking, she said, "I'm sorry if you felt uncomfortable. Poppy can help you move to another room."

Lea peered at Ivy in earnest. "Do you think I'm being silly, or worse, might be a little unhinged?"

Ivy pressed a hand to her shoulder. "Not at all. I believe you." A look passed between them, and Lea slowly nodded. *She knows, just like I do.* "But if you sensed something, I would venture to say it's friendly, wouldn't you?"

Getting hold of herself again, Lea exhaled. "Yes, more curious than anything."

"Some of us are more sensitive than others. Do you want to move rooms, though?" Ivy smiled in encouragement. "A clean start will help you rest better."

Grinning, Lea said, "That would be a good idea."

The two women strolled back to the inn together, and Lea asked a few questions about the inn.

Ivy answered her and then said, "I'm happy to give you that tour when you're ready."

Lea quickly agreed.

Ivy sensed something about this woman. She liked her, and she could see that she was sensitive. But was there more to her story than she imagined? Ivy wasn't sure, but she intended to find out.

9

*B*ennett returned from his morning run on the beach and rushed through his shower. As he dressed, he noticed the door to Ivy's closet standing open in their bedroom. On the inside of the door hung a dress the color of cotton candy, its fabric frothy and light. He hesitated, trying to picture that on Ivy, but the result was incongruent at best.

Ivy was getting dressed for the day ahead, too.

"Is that your new dress for the gala?" he asked.

"That's the one." Ivy slipped into a pair of dark jeans, her expression a mixture of resolve and faint resignation. With its ruffled tiers, the dress seemed out of place, more suited to a sweet sixteen party than a sophisticated seaside gala, especially for a woman of Ivy's poise and grace.

"That's interesting," Bennett began, his tone careful. "It's a unique choice for the gala."

"You can say what you're thinking." Ivy glanced over her shoulder with a wry expression. "It's very pink, very fluffy, and very not me. But it's what I found, and it will have to work."

"It's not too late to find something you like."

She curved up a corner of her mouth. "I know it looks like something out of a teen prom catalog. In fact, I think I wore something like that. If I can channel my seventeen-year-old self, I'll be fine."

"Then why settle for it?" he asked, furrowing his brow. He couldn't quite reconcile the dress with the woman he knew. Shelly, maybe. For Halloween. But Ivy? No way.

Ivy slipped on a crisp white shirt and stepped into stylish silver sneakers. "The thrift shop didn't have much selection, and with the gala so close, there's no time for alterations. We have so much to do, and I'm still working on sketches to enter into the auction. Every penny we can raise counts." She met his gaze, a glint of humor in her determined eyes. "It's not ideal, but it will do. The truth is, I started too late. But I accept it."

Bennett knew Ivy was practical, often putting the inn and their family's needs above hers. Yet, he hated to think of her compromising, especially at such a memorable event.

He also felt guilty about his new suit hanging in the closet.

"You should have something you feel amazing in," he said, the image of her in that pink confection clashing with his vision of her enjoying the elegant evening.

Ivy fastened a small silver chain around her neck and looked up, her expression resolute. "It's just one night. What is important is the fundraiser and preserving a historic piece of Summer Beach. Not what I wear. I wish people would just forget this." She sliced her hands out. "It's fine, and that's that."

He understood, of course. Yet, with his new Italian evening suit hanging in the closet, he couldn't shake the feeling of imbalance.

"I just picked up a new suit." His confession left a taste of guilt in his mouth. "Now I wish I'd gone to the thrift shop with you instead."

Ivy looked at him with a wry expression. "You in an ill-fitting secondhand tux wouldn't be right. You're the leader of Summer Beach. Don't feel bad." She threaded silver hoop earrings through her pierced earlobes as she spoke. "We play the hand we're dealt, which sometimes includes a fluffy pink dress." Gesturing toward the dress, she added, "I promise that will be the last time you'll ever see it."

Bennett's heart swelled with love for this woman who handled challenging situations with creative solutions, but he still had his doubts.

"That dress will look different with the right shoes and accessories." Ivy wrapped her arms around him. "I appreciate your understanding, but let's make a deal—no photos to immortalize my prom queen moment."

"How about from the neck up only?"

Ivy kissed him. "That I can live with."

The gala would come and go, but moments like this, with the love of his life in his arms, were the ones that counted.

"I have to run," Ivy said, picking up a bright jacket.

"Tomato-red; now that's a good color on you. Let me help you with that." Bennett took the jacket and held it for her.

Ivy slid her arms through and smiled. "I like to think of it as lipstick-red."

"Oh, you don't like the food description? I guess that's the difference between men and women." He kissed her again. "Busy day?"

"Always," she said, looking at him with the smile that always warmed his heart. "How about you?"

"Same." He spared her the details. Mitch had asked for his help today at noon, but everything else at work was more of the same. "I'll see you after work."

After a busy morning at City Hall, Bennett took a lunch break. Once at Java Beach, he opened the door to the familiar sound of beach reggae and the scent of freshly ground coffee beans. Mitch's place was usually busy, and today was no exception. People were ordering the salads and paninis he'd added to the lunch menu.

Mitch spotted him immediately. With a wave and a wide grin, he cut through the crowd. "That Arlo dude is over there, man. He's the guy in the blue." He gestured to a corner table where two men sat with their backs to him. "Thanks for backing me up on this. Shelly insisted, but it feels weird. Like an interview."

Bennett chuckled. "I've got your back."

But as he approached the table, his apprehension grew. The pair wore sports jackets with light trousers and loafers. That was casual in many places, but they looked overdressed for Summer Beach. They were in their forties, about his age.

The idea that one of these men was dating Poppy didn't sit well with him. It wasn't just the age difference that bothered him.

The one closest to him turned to the side, and Bennett clenched his jaw with dismay. It was Wyatt, the one rumored to run against him in the upcoming election. That was still months away, but this guy could sow a lot of discord in that time.

Of all people to be talking to the guy they were going to meet.

Bennett paused, steeling himself for the encounter.

Mitch returned with a tray of coffee. "Thought we might need a jolt. Did you see who's there?"

"Is Wyatt already working on voters?"

"No, Arlo introduced him as a friend," Mitch replied. "I swear I had no idea."

Bennett clenched his jaw. "Then let's make this quick." Instantly, his blood pressure spiked.

Mitch made the introductions. "Bennett, this is Arlo, and you know Wyatt. Guys, Bennett is Poppy's uncle by marriage."

"And the current mayor," Wyatt said, jutting his jaw.

The men exchanged handshakes. Wyatt's grip was firm

and challenging, while Arlo's was confident. Bennett maintained his composure though his mind simmered with protective instincts.

Looking uncomfortable with the small talk, Mitch turned to Arlo. "What brings you to Summer Beach?"

"My old buddy is here now, and since I'm seeing Poppy, it makes sense."

Mitch nodded. "You're, uh, living in L.A.?"

"I have family here, too," Arlo replied.

Wyatt cut in, lacing his fingers and grinning. "Am I the next to be interrogated, Ben?"

"It's Bennett. And I'm not interested in you, Wyatt."

"No? Even though I'm dating your stepdaughter?"

"You're *what?*" Bennett rose from his chair, but Mitch pulled him down. Everyone had turned to look, and it was all Bennett could do to restrain himself. Pointing a finger at Wyatt, he gritted his teeth. "You're a creep, you know that? She's half your age. Does she know you're planning to run against me this year?"

Wyatt grinned. "That hasn't come up yet, but only because I haven't filed the official papers. But I suppose you'll break the news early for me."

Acutely aware of the tables surrounding them, Bennett stared at Wyatt. He kept his voice low and even. "You're dating her to irritate me, and if you think that will throw me off my game, you don't know me very well. But about Sunny—"

"Hey, chill." Wyatt held up his hands. "I swear that had nothing to do with it. But it will make for an interesting race. I wonder who she'll choose?"

The mayoral race had just taken a very personal turn. Before Bennett could think of a civil reply, Mitch cleared his throat and steered the conversation back to Arlo.

"Look, I don't have anything against you," Mitch began, sliding his gaze toward Wyatt. "Except maybe your choice of friends. I don't know you, but Poppy said you're moving fast, and she wanted us to meet before she introduced you to her parents."

Arlo looked surprised. "Whoa. I didn't say anything about meeting her parents. I asked her to stay with me in L.A., that's all. She's the one moving fast."

Mitch leaned forward. In a measured voice, he said, "Whatever. You're a little old for her, but if you want to be with Poppy, you get us, too. We're a close family, and we look out for each other. You got that?"

Mitch had put Arlo on notice. Bennett held his anger in check.

"Look, I thought she was older," Arlo replied. "Poppy is mature for her age, and she handles herself well. I don't think she needs you guys running interference. I thought you wanted to talk to me about a business proposition."

"So, that's what she told you," Mitch said. "Well, this is family business then."

"See, age is just a number," Wyatt added, meeting Bennett's gaze directly, a smug edge to his smile. "What matters is the connection, the spark. Don't you think Sunny's mother would agree?"

"Now you're asking for it," Bennett said, rising again. Mayor or not, he had to protect Ivy and Sunny from a guy like this.

"Hey, there," Mitch said, pulling him down again.

Just then, Bennett caught a glimpse of the red jacket he'd helped Ivy with this morning. She and Shelly were slipping through the rear beach entrance. They tucked themselves behind a potted plant and kept their sunglasses on, as if they were spies on a mission.

Bennett grimaced. They had the worst timing.

But then, the moment Shelly spied Arlo, her mouth dropped open.

Mitch, oblivious to Shelly's presence, leaned in. "Look,

Arlo, Bennett and I will make sure you treat Poppy and Sunny right—or you get us. They're adults, but they're family. You know as well as I do how young women are exploited. That's not happening here. Got it?"

Suddenly, Shelly abandoned her hideout and approached them. Her face was a mask of barely concealed disgust. She glared at Arlo. "What are you doing talking to my husband?"

Mitch looked surprised. "I didn't think you knew Arlo."

"Is that what you're calling yourself now?" Shelly smirked. "What, did you wear out the name Grant?"

Arlo bristled at that. "It's A. Grant Jackson, remember? A is for Arlo." However, his confidence faltered, and he shifted uncomfortably. "Shelly, I swear I didn't know that Poppy was any relation to you."

"That's a lie. I told you we ran Seabreeze Inn. Don't even think about going to the gala with your mother." Shelly's eyes blazed into him. "If you touch Poppy again, you'll have me to deal with, and you know how ugly that can get."

Bennett thrust out his hands. "This meeting is over. We all know where we stand." If it went on any longer, they'd all be fodder for gossip—if they weren't already.

Shelly raised a finger to Arlo. "I mean it. Stay away from my niece."

Ivy raced toward Shelly. "What's going on?"

"We're through here, that's what." Bennett took her by the hand. "Let's go."

Mitch could deal with Shelly. With a last warning glance at Wyatt, Bennett quickly steered Ivy from the cafe. Once outside, she whipped around. "What was that all about?"

He took her hand, wondering how to break this to her. "That was Wyatt, the guy planning to run against me."

She looked perplexed. "Why was he with Arlo? Or Grant, or whoever that jerk is."

Bennett pushed a hand through his hair. "That's where it gets complicated. I'm afraid he's dating Sunny."

"That guy?" she blurted out.

Bennett drew his hands over his face in frustration. "We need to talk with her. Or you two alone. Whatever you want, but Sunny needs to know who she's dealing with. He hasn't told her about his plan to run against me."

"Unbelievable. Oh, Sunny. How could you?" Ivy threw up her hands. "If I say anything, she's likely to take it wrong."

"Then we can talk to her together. Maybe if it's coming from me, it will help." Seeing her face, he took her hands. "Come with me. We both need to get out here and cool off."

As they hurried to his SUV, Bennett considered the situation. Sunny might be mercurial, but he still trusted that she could be reasonable. After all, when he and Ivy were on their honeymoon, Sunny had tackled her problems and prevailed. She was growing up, maybe not in a linear manner, but in fits and spurts, as they all had. And making a few mistakes along the way.

Bennett helped Ivy into the car, and she sat looking dazed, angry, and upset. Sunny had made a big error in judgment, not that she had been aware of Wyatt's true game. The guy had put one over on them. Now, no one would get out of this without being hurt.

10

"*A*re you enjoying your new room?" Ivy asked. Poppy had helped Lea move from the old one, which had made Lea uncomfortable.

"It's just as nice, thank you," Lea replied. " And I've changed my mind about what happened. I might have overreacted." A faraway look filled Lea's eyes. "If we're not expecting someone to reach out to us, it can be a surprise. Like a friend we haven't heard from in a long time. I'm much better now."

"As long as you're comfortable," Ivy said, relieved to hear this. Her heart went out to Lea. She liked her, and they'd had a good talk on the beach.

Today, Ivy had enough on her mind with Sunny and Poppy and the entire gala that needed to come together. Time was running short, yet she had promised Lea a tour.

The morning sun shone through the windows as Ivy led Lea through the ballroom, where tables were set up for the gala.

Lea's gaze lingered on the chandeliers and architectural features. "It's beautiful," she murmured. "Will you be able to restore the entire place with the funds you raise from the gala?"

"Along with other grants and tax credits," Ivy replied. "It's complicated, but we worked it out with someone specializing in historical properties. As long as we meet our auction goals at the gala, we should be able to complete the restoration."

Lea touched the mantle with reverence. "I'm pleased you're saving this home. Its history is important to the community. And to many people," she quickly added. "Your family, I'm sure."

"We love living here and hosting people." Ivy thought about how much this old beach house meant to her.

Lea's face brightened with curiosity. "May I see where Amelia hid the paintings?"

"Sure, this way." Ivy led her downstairs. She enjoyed sharing the excitement she and Shelly felt when they discovered this section of the house. "This passageway was sealed off for decades."

"Do you know why Amelia might have done that?" Lea asked as they descended.

"We think she was frightened or traumatized by events she experienced earlier in her life," Ivy replied. "We found receipts for building materials she purchased right after the attack on Pearl Harbor. Since then, we understand that she hid the artwork for safety, not trusting anyone until she could reunite the paintings with their rightful owners."

Ivy paused at the bottom of the stairway for Lea to look around. "During the war, Amelia transformed the house into a center for rehabilitation for service members. Even after the war ended, the work here continued for some time. And, given that communication was difficult, she might not have been able to locate previous owners of the artwork still concealed."

"That was too often the case," Lea said with a trace of sadness. "Where exactly did you find the paintings?"

"Right over here." Ivy showed her the spot and told her about the art pieces and antique furnishings that had been stored. "We believe Amelia saved as many paintings as she could."

"That sounds like something she would have done," Lea said softly. "She and her father cared so much about artists."

Ivy inclined her head. Lea spoke as if she was familiar with them. "Have you read much about the Ericksons or Amelia's father?"

"They were fascinating," Lea replied with a slow nod, although she didn't elaborate. "May I see the attic area where she sheltered people?"

Ivy was pleased that Lea wanted to see that area, too. "That discovery meant more to us than the art she saved, although it wasn't reported much in the news." Ivy was a little surprised that she knew about that. Lea must have read Shelly's blog about it or seen one of her videos. "This way."

Ivy climbed the stairs to the second story. "We created new access to the attic here. When we found this area, the only way in was through a rear panel of a closet inside Amelia Erickson's bedroom. We've renovated the space to accommodate guests but also wanted to preserve images of what we found."

Ivy gestured to photos and sketches on the walls before climbing the next flight of stairs they had installed to the attic rooms.

"There's not much to see anymore," Ivy said, opening the door to one guest room. "These rooms didn't have windows, so we added them for ventilation and light."

Lea took in everything with a sense of awe. "Thank you for letting me see this."

"Would you like to see an old photo album? They held many parties here."

Lea's face lit with delight. "I would love to. I didn't know you had photos. Are they of her family, too?"

"Possibly," Ivy said. "We're not sure who most people are in the photos, aside from the obvious historical figures.

We've been learning as we go and finding bits and pieces. A few journal pages, Christmas ornaments, even a wedding dress."

Lea looked like she could burst with excitement. "Would it be too much trouble for me to see everything?"

Ivy hesitated. They didn't usually bring everything out for guests to see, but those items might also be an excellent addition to the gala. "You've given me an idea. We could organize a display of the items we've found."

"I would be happy to help," Lea said, nearly breathless with excitement.

"We'll let you know." Ivy led the way downstairs. She brought out the old photo album and placed it on a table so Lea could look through it. When she opened the old album, Lea gasped.

"I never imagined I would see anything like this," Lea said. "Would you mind if I took photos? Only for personal use, I promise. I love history."

"I suppose that's okay," Ivy said. That made her a little uncomfortable, but as it was only for Lea's personal enjoyment, she couldn't deny the request. Still, Lea seemed so eager. "You're quite the historian. What did you say brought you all this way?"

Lea blushed and dipped her head. "I've asked too many questions, haven't I?"

"No," Ivy replied slowly. Maybe Lea wrote for a news outlet, or she was writing a book. "But you seem like you're on a quest. Are you writing a story about the Ericksons?"

Lea looked up from the album. "I wasn't sure how to tell you, but my grandmother left a few letters for me shortly before she died. They were left to her by her mother and sent to her by an older sister I'd never heard about. We didn't talk about the war very much."

Ivy tried to follow the connection. "What is the relation to the Ericksons?"

"Not both of them," Lea replied. "Only Amelia. She was my great-grandmother Ursula's older half-sister."

This struck Ivy. "Are you sure?"

"I've confirmed the story with my grandmother's friends, who knew she'd been adopted as a young child during the war. Amelia and Ursula were related through their father, Hans, who was head of a museum in Berlin. After the death of his first wife—Amelia's mother—he remarried and had my grandmother. She was their only child."

As Ivy pieced together this new information, she gestured toward a photo in the album of Amelia and Gustav. With a sinking feeling, she recalled the provision Bennett once mentioned in Amelia's will and trust. The property had to be held for a certain number of years in case a niece could be located.

Was that niece one of Lea's ancestors?

Ivy pushed aside the thought and turned back to Lea. "We've often wondered what happened to Amelia's father. Do you know?"

With a small sigh, Lea touched the edge of the photo. "He and his wife Ursula died during the war. One family friend said there was a rumor that he'd diverted artwork earmarked for destruction, and he was arrested for helping artists escape. I don't know if that was true, but they disappeared."

"That's terribly sad," Ivy said thoughtfully. "But their child survived?"

"They hid her with friends," Lea replied. "She was too young to have any memory of what happened. Not even memories of her parents."

Ivy nodded, taking the story in. "This is why you came then."

"I had to," Lea said. "Learning about Amelia, even if she was only a half-sister to my great-grandmother, means so much to me. To see where and how she lived is something I've been looking forward to. That's all I could think of when I saw a notice of your gala event."

"Maybe we'll find some older photos of their father in here." Ivy imagined how much meaning that would have to Lea. "I'm glad you came, and we're happy to share what we know of her." Ivy turned a brittle page in the album with care. "From the photos they took, they enjoyed giving parties."

"How beautifully dressed they were." Lea looked closely at the images. "Do you mind if I ask, how did you and your husband acquire this home?"

From her question, Ivy knew she had read newspaper articles about the paintings. Lea undoubtedly had access to a wealth of research material online.

"Actually, the newspapers had it wrong," Ivy said. "My husband bought this house before he died. I didn't know anything about it."

A smile touched Lea's lips. "He planned to surprise you?"

"It was certainly a shock but not what he intended." Ivy shook her head. "That's a story for another day."

Lea scanned Ivy's face. "Did your husband buy it from the Erickson's other heirs?"

Ivy noted how the younger woman phrased her question. Was that a slip? "They didn't have any," she replied.

Lea was quiet for a moment. "No other family?"

A flutter of caution stirred within Ivy, and she wondered if Lea was trying to ascertain who might have inherited the Erickson's property.

Ivy cleared her throat to reply. "This house and another one in San Francisco that Viola Standish owns were in Amelia's estate. Her husband Gustav had passed away years earlier. The proceeds from her estate benefited several charities she had named in her will."

Lea absorbed this information without any sign of emotion. "I see. I'd like to know more about that. To know what sort of causes she valued."

"I'm afraid I don't know." Ivy didn't, but still, she felt a little guilty for not sharing the entire story. Had Lea returned to claim part of the estate? A moment of panic set in, yet she hated thinking that way. The other woman had given her no reason to suspect her of that.

Or had she?

Ivy was struggling to understand how all these new pieces fit into the puzzle of Amelia's life. "You said that Amelia wrote to your great-grandmother, although she was only a little girl then?"

"When you read them, you'll understand. I brought the letters with me. Would you like to see them later?"

"Yes, I would. Why don't you have dinner with my family and me tonight, and you can share them then?"

"I'd like that very much." Lea looked down at the photo album. "I have so much admiration for Amelia and all that she did. Do you mind if I stay here and look at these photos for a while?"

Although Ivy was a little nervous, she agreed. "Just be careful with them. They're quite old and fragile. If you need anything, I'll be in the ballroom helping my sister prepare for the gala."

They agreed to meet before dinner. In the meantime, Ivy's mind was a whirl of questions. What connection did Lea really want to have with this house? She had traveled a long way at great expense to look at photos and take a tour of the place. Ivy didn't know anything about her, only what Lea had told her.

Ivy left her guest to look over the old photos and went to the ballroom, where she began tidying before Shelly arrived.

Despite her reservations, Ivy was curious. The house tour had taken an unexpected turn. The letters Lea carried with her might provide another thread in the intricate tapestry of Amelia's history.

Another thought occurred to her. Whatever Lea's intent,

Ivy had to share this development with Viola. The terms of the will covering her home in San Francisco were the same as for the Las Brisas del Mar.

And, as Meredith had once told her, Viola Standish was not a woman one trifled with.

Ivy dreaded making that call, but she knew she must. First, however, she needed more information from Lea. The letters she had might well impact the terms of the will if Amelia had made any promises to Lea's grandmother.

Ivy wondered what that might mean for all of them, Viola included.

$\mathcal{I}$vy was sorting decorations with Shelly at the dining room table when she heard footsteps. Poppy was out running errands. Ivy looked up, but it was their neighbor, Darla, her sparkly visor catching the sunlight that streamed through into the ballroom.

"There's my sweet grandbaby." Darla held her arms to Daisy, who cooed with delight when she saw her. "We're going to spend the afternoon together to let your mother and auntie work."

"Granny Darla is here," Shelly said, scooping up Daisy with one hand and tucking the diaper bag under the other arm.

Ivy smiled at the exchange between Shelly and Darla, however unlikely it might have been at one time. When Ivy and Shelly had landed here in Summer Beach, neither of them could have imagined their cranky neighbor would have ever been on friendly terms with them, let alone virtually adopting Shelly's child as her grandchild.

Darla considered Mitch one of her own. Her son had died years before, and Mitch was no longer in contact with his parents, who weren't usually on the right side of the law. She was a regular at Java Beach, and Mitch saw through her cranky nature. He once told Shelly his mission had been to get a smile out of Darla.

"Now that's she's crawling, I've baby-proofed my house," Darla said, planting a kiss on Daisy's pink cheek. "She'll be safe there, and I'll watch her every minute."

Giggling with joy, Daisy reached for Darla's crystal-encrusted visor.

"Oh, you little rascal." She hugged Daisy to her chest. "We'll have so much fun. I have finger painting all set up for you. Then you'll have a bubble bath because you'll probably paint yourself in the process."

"I'm sure she will," Shelly said. "She's fed and ready to go. What happens at Granny's, stays at Granny's—as long as Daisy returns in one piece."

Behind them, Poppy walked into the dining room and laughed. "You're pretty chill, Aunt Shelly."

"So was your mom," Shelly said. "At least, after the first one. I figured I'd start with that attitude. See you in a few hours." She kissed the top of Daisy's head and sent them off.

"You just made Darla's day," Ivy said. "She thought she'd never have grandchildren."

"We help each other." Shelly gazed through the open doors after Darla, who was bustling next door. "Why not spread the love around? We're lucky on my side, but Mitch and I have decided that family is who we say it is."

Ivy beamed at her sister. "I'm proud of you two for that."

"Maybe I'm finally growing up. I guess that's what kids do to a person." Shelly chuckled. "Now I know why you're like you are."

"Hey, you." Ivy swatted her.

Shelly burst out laughing. "Just kidding, Ives."

"I knew that," Ivy said, grinning. "Now, tell me what to do for these fancy centerpieces."

Shelly gestured toward the supplies she'd brought. "We'll start with this stuff. I have a plan."

"What about the flowers?" Poppy asked.

Shelly shook her head. "It's too soon. I'll buy them wholesale from the Los Angeles Flower Market the day before the event. I'll have to leave here at four in the morning to get the best selection, but given how much we need, it will be worth it."

"Okay, let's get started," Ivy said, sitting down again to help. She saw Shelly eyeing Poppy. This was the first time they'd been alone with Poppy since the fiasco at Java Beach with Arlo and Wyatt. Sunny had been avoiding her, too.

Shelly glanced at their niece. "Hey, Poppy. Did Arlo tell you about his meeting with Mitch?"

Poppy looked up, surprised. "He didn't say a word. They've already met? All he said was that he'd been busy lately."

When Shelly shot a questioning look at Ivy, she nodded. Poppy needed to know about Arlo—or Grant. Whatever name he was going by.

Shelly reached for Poppy's hand. "Sweetie, there's something we have to tell you about Arlo. I'm afraid you're not going to like it."

Ivy leaned in. "Shelly knew him when they both lived in New York. They used to date."

Poppy's mouth opened in shock. "Why didn't you tell me, Aunt Shelly?"

"He went by Grant in New York. I guess Arlo is cooler now. I had no idea until Ivy and I went to spy on the guys' meeting at Java Beach."

Looking confused at this revelation, Poppy sat back. "Why hasn't he told me this?"

"Because he's only out for himself," Shelly said, reaching for her hand. "He's not good enough for you. I'm so sorry."

"But his phone calls, and the flowers... I thought Arlo

really liked me. He wanted to make plans together." Tears welled in her eyes.

Ivy jumped up, brought a tissue box back from the powder room, and handed it to Poppy. Sniffling, her niece took a tissue and wiped her eyes.

Shelly told her a little of his past, and Poppy listened, not saying anything.

Ivy's heart went out to their poor niece. "Were you really falling for him, sweetheart?"

Poppy nodded sadly. "He acted like he adored me, and that can be addictive. When I think about it now, he was love-bombing me. What did he want from me?"

"Just you, darling," Ivy said. "You're a beautiful young woman any man would be proud to have and show off. Some men are like that. I'm afraid he didn't have your best interests at heart."

"How could you tell?" Poppy asked.

Shelly looked at her niece with a pained expression. "When you've been out with as many jerks as I have, you can see them coming. You have to rely on your instincts, which were correct. You were worried about introducing him to your parents, and you were dead right about that."

"You'll know when you find the right guy," Ivy added. "Unfortunately, it's often hard to know when they're wrong, especially when they come on that strong."

"Thank you for telling me." Poppy hugged them both. "Now I have to break it off."

Ivy embraced her. "If you want to talk about it, we're always here."

Poppy wiped her eyes again. "Did you tell Sunny?"

"I haven't caught up with her yet," Ivy replied. "Would you rather tell her?"

Poppy nodded. "I would."

After another hug, they continued sorting the ribbons and other accessories that Shelly had selected. While they worked, they took breaks to tend to calls and guest questions but still made good headway.

After lunch, they sat down again to continue, and Ivy thought Poppy looked better. Their niece sat down and grinned.

"Well, I did it," Poppy announced. "I called Arlo and broke up."

Shelly let out a sigh of relief. "Thank goodness. How did he take it?"

"Basically, he told me I'd never find another man like him. When he started in on you, Aunt Shelly, I hung up on him." Poppy made the sign of an L with her thumb and forefinger. "He's a big loser. Next."

Shelly chuckled, and Ivy was relieved. "Dating disaster averted. Good for you."

They continued working, and while Shelly and Poppy chatted, Ivy thought about Lea. The younger woman was thrilled to find an ancestor in Amelia, and she seemed nice enough, but the terms of Amelia's old will concerned Ivy. She wondered what was in the letters that had survived.

Had any promises been made in those? Ivy glanced at the time. Dinner was still a few hours away, but this was all she could think of.

Across from her, Shelly began filling tall cylinders with blue stones and natural shells. She paused and peered at Ivy. "Okay, your turn, Ives. Want to tell us what's on your mind?"

Ivy blew out a breath. "Is it that obvious?"

"When you're not talking about what's next on that perpetual list in your mind, I know something's up."

Slowly, Ivy nodded. "I took Lea on a tour of the house. It was enlightening."

Poppy lowered her voice. "I knew something was up when I saw you two in the parlor looking through the old photos. Lea seemed pretty emotional."

Ivy unwound a length of blue ribbon, fashioning large bows for the centerpieces as she spoke. Quickly, she shared what Lea had told her.

Shelly clamped a hand to her mouth. "Wait a minute, her grandmother was the *niece*?"

"Or half-niece?" Ivy wasn't sure what to call her.

"Would that make her a half-grand-niece?" Poppy asked. "Or would that be a half-double-grand?"

"Sounds like you're ordering coffee," Shelly said. "Whatever she is, do you think she's here to check out the place before filing a claim?"

Ivy ran a hand over her face. "The time allowed has long passed, but does that matter? She shouldn't be cheated out of an inheritance because of a missed deadline."

"That's how these things work, Ives." Shelly made a face. "Convenient that she turns up after all the work and money that's been poured into this place. It's probably worth twice what it was. Please tell me you won't return this place like you did the paintings and jewels we found."

Shelly and Poppy exchanged a worried look.

In truth, Ivy was concerned, too. "This couldn't have happened at a worse time. I don't know how to tell Viola or what to do."

"Do nothing," Shelly said, snipping a tall curly willow. "Just go ahead with what you've planned. If Lea thinks she has a right to anything, you'll hear from lawyers soon enough."

Ivy winced at the thought. Just when she thought her troubles with this old house might be easing.

"I think Aunt Shelly is right," Poppy said. "Whatever the ownership is, the house is on the historical list and needs saving. Let's get through the event and see what happens."

Ivy gave them a sad smile. "If nothing else, this will be our grand finale."

"Probably not," Shelly said, putting her arm around Ivy.

"You don't know what she wants yet. Maybe she really is here to soak in the ambiance about her ancestors—and nothing more."

Ivy rested her head on Shelly's shoulder. "You're usually the cynical one. I'm surprised."

Shelly hugged her tightly. "Maybe you've taught me there's another way. Come on, we don't have long to turn this into a magical mermaid setting."

That was true. Other guests would be arriving soon. Ivy planned to call Viola tomorrow, once she learned more from Lea tonight.

She tried to push thoughts of Lea from her mind and busy herself with the decorating scheme Shelly had developed. They had a lot of work to do.

Ivy watched as her sister took the lead. Shelly had worked on many such events in New York.

Working together, they draped the round tables in aquamarine cloths and prepared Shelly's bold centerpieces. Flowers would be added later.

Ivy enjoyed watching everything come together. They were all filled with purpose as they unpacked old shells and decorations from Amelia's collection, items that hadn't seen the light of day in decades.

They filled the long table for the silent auction with donated items from the community and Viola's VIP list. In the center were reserved spots for Carol Reston's framed autographed music and lyric sheets.

The vintage diamond necklace from Amelia's grandmother would be the crown jewel of the event, resting under a center spotlight.

When they finished, Ivy lowered the lights. Shelly's silver touches glowed under the chandeliers. Ivy was pleased with how much they accomplished in an afternoon.

A low whistle filled the air. "What a transformation,"

Bennett said as he strolled into the room. He put his arm around Ivy and kissed her.

"This is Shelly's vision," Ivy said.

"We all pitched in," Shelly added.

Ivy checked the time and frowned. "Have you seen Sunny? She promised to take care of the wine and tea hour this evening."

Poppy glanced down, and Ivy wondered if Sunny was out with that man Wyatt. Ivy shuddered at the thought. She still needed to talk with Sunny about that, but her daughter had been making herself scarce, dashing out in the morning and returning after Ivy had gone to bed. She hoped Sunny was getting her work done on her paper.

"She just got home, and I saw her race into the music room," Bennett added softly. "Trust her to manage it."

Sunny needed to work on her paper after dinner. Ivy wouldn't say anything, though. Her daughter knew what she needed to do.

Bennett interrupted her thoughts. "Ivy, shouldn't you be working on your sketches of Amelia tonight? People will want to see them at the auction."

She had shared the idea with him. "I have to make dinner. I invited our guest Lea because she has some old letters she wants to share." Quickly, she filled him in.

"Then let me take care of dinner," he said, smoothing her hair from her forehead. "You can take a couple of hours to work."

Encouraged by his support, Ivy felt a surge of creative energy. "Have I told you you're the best husband ever?"

"Right back at you, sweetheart." Bennett waved his hand. "I'll pitch in here and then make dinner."

With a final glance at the bustling activity in the ballroom, Ivy made her way to her studio at the rear of the house. This space was her only sanctuary and where her creativity could flourish. At this time of day, bright natural light filled the room.

She slipped an oversized work shirt over her blouse, opened a pad of textured paper, and picked up her charcoal. She planned to sketch a few ideas before creating a larger work for the auction.

As she began to sketch, her mind wandered through the stories she knew of Amelia's life, each line on the paper a tribute to the woman who had left indelible marks on this home and the lives she touched.

Amelia had sheltered friends and strangers alike, including a member of Ivy's family, Carlotta's aunt, who suffered an accident in the final stage of her pregnancy.

She let her charcoal glide across the paper, sketching the strong profile of Amelia's face filled with purpose. On another page, she outlined the house and the ocean beyond.

The time flew, and soon, a tap sounded at the door. Looking up, Ivy saw that it was almost time for dinner. The smell of food wound through her open windows.

"Be right there," she called out.

With some reluctance, she put away her tools. It took time to immerse herself in her work, but she had become accustomed to short sessions. As long as she kept to a schedule, she could still produce what she needed for the gallery.

Expecting to see Bennett or Sunny, she opened the door and was immediately surprised. "Oh, hello, Lea."

"I hope I'm not disturbing you." In her hand, the other woman clutched a few envelopes yellowed with age. "I overheard your daughter telling another guest you were working in your studio, so I asked where it was. Sunny seemed a little reluctant to say. I'm afraid I pressed her."

"It's time I quit for the evening anyway." She wiped charcoal dust from her hands. "Will you still join us for dinner?"

The younger woman nodded. "I appreciate your invitation."

Ivy noticed Lea's demeanor had changed from earlier this afternoon. The weight of whatever she carried on her shoulders was evident in her downcast eyes.

"Lea, is everything alright?" Ivy asked, removing her stained work shirt.

"I've been thinking about my mother and grandmother, and how they would have liked to see all this." Lea heaved a sigh. "But they've both passed on."

"I'm so sorry. Do you have other family?"

She shook her head. "No blood relatives at all."

Ivy realized she didn't know if Lea was married or involved. "Do you have a boyfriend or someone special in your life?"

A smile curved Lea's lips. "My wedding is next month. Michael is working, so he couldn't join me here, but I didn't want to miss this gala. I didn't know when I might be able to visit again."

"And what does your Michael do?"

"He helps run a family business. We met at university but didn't date. Years later, we reconnected at a class reunion. The timing was right."

Ivy was happy that Lea wasn't alone in the world. "Your life will soon change. I'm sure your mother would be very proud of you."

"I like to think so," Lea said with a trace of sadness. "My mother died when I was young, and I never knew my father."

"I'm sorry to hear that, but it seems like you have a bright future ahead."

"Oh, yes. I certainly do." Lea hesitated. "I want to know who I really am before I marry. You see, my ancestry was practically lost. Then, stories my grandmother told me began to make sense. I stumbled across an article about the masterpieces you discovered here and realized the stories I'd heard were true." She held out the letters. "I want to read these to you."

Ivy touched Lea's sleeve. "May we do that after dinner? I've shared what you told me with my husband and my sister. They're interested, too. And it smells like our supper is ready."

Lea agreed, and they went outside. Ivy saw Mitch setting up a long table on the veranda. Bennett was tending the grill. Shelly sat on a chaise lounge, nursing Daisy. Even Sunny was there putting napkins and plates on the table.

Ivy was glad her family was there with her for moral support. She sensed that Lea's story would illuminate another part of Amelia and her home's history.

More than that, it might change the course of their lives again—and on the eve of the gala meant to free them from worry.

12

"*D*inner is ready," Bennett called out, brandishing a steel spatula over the barbecue. "Line up, and I'll dish out."

"Guests first," Ivy said to Lea. "We're pretty casual here."

Bennett had grilled salmon and veggies. "Hope you're hungry. Mitch brought a salad and chocolate chip cookies for dessert from Java Beach."

After everyone had been served and taken their seat, Ivy kissed her husband. "Thanks for making dinner. I needed some time to myself."

"I could see that," Bennett replied, placing grilled fish and vegetables on her plate.

Sunny appeared beside her. "Mom, I have to work on my paper for school tonight, so I'm going to eat and run."

"We need to talk, sweetheart."

"I know, that's why I'm telling you this. I'm not avoiding you, but I have to get this work done." Sunny paused, suddenly self-conscious. "You were right; I should have stayed home and started earlier. Sometimes it's hard to say no."

"I just want you to know who you're dealing with."

Chewing her lip, Sunny glanced away. "Poppy told me she broke up with Arlo."

Even though her daughter had avoided the question, Ivy felt a guarded sense of relief. "I know it can be hard to keep priorities straight, so I'm proud of you." She didn't need to mention Wyatt right now. That could wait until later.

Sunny gave her a quick smile of relief. "Thanks, Mom."

The sun was low in the sky, and an early evening ocean breeze swept around them. Ivy sat down, feeling grateful for her family gathered around the table.

Bennett placed the rest of the food on the table with a crisp salad and warm bread. He had been experimenting with herb-infused olive oils, so he passed those around, too.

Ivy loved their impromptu family meals. She poured lemon-infused water for everyone and wine for those who wanted it. The conversation at the table revolved around the upcoming gala and items they had found in the old inn.

Lea listened intently to the conversation. "What was the last thing you found?" she asked.

"Just an old address book." Yet, even as Ivy replied, she realized the value that might have to Lea. While everyone in that book had likely passed on, maybe she could track families of old friends—or even distant relatives.

From the look Shelly sent her across the table, she must have had the same thought. But before Ivy said anything more, they needed to examine the addresses.

After eating, Sunny excused herself. Ivy would fill her in later.

When everyone had finished, Ivy asked, "Lea, would you like to share your connection to Amelia Erickson?"

Lea brought out the letters and placed them on the table as she spoke. "These three letters are ones that Amelia wrote to my grandmother, Hannah. They were half-sisters, and it seemed Amelia was trying to entertain her. What comes through in the letters is also her warmth and appreciation for my great-grandmother Ursula, who married Amelia's father, Hans. I think they were friends because they weren't that far apart in age."

Ivy was already fascinated. "He presided over an art museum, didn't he?"

"He did," Lea replied. "And I believe he ultimately gave his life for his love of art. Not that he planned it that way, of course."

"I can understand his commitment," Ivy said, feeling a reassuring touch of Bennett's hand on hers.

"Would you mind reading the letters?" Ivy asked as Mitch served mugs of tea and passed around cookies.

"They're not too long," Lea said. "She was writing to a child, after all." She sipped from her glass of water and began translating as she read. "Dearest little Hannah…"

Lea read the letters, which contained simple observances about the ocean, shell collecting, local wildlife, and how much she enjoyed her beach house.

Ivy imagined Amelia sitting on the veranda, maybe where they were now. "She must have written that letter from here."

The other letter was similar, but she wrote about San Francisco.

Ivy had an idea. "May I see the envelopes?"

Lea handed them to her, and Ivy looked at the addresses with interest. The return address was a postal box in Summer Beach, likely at the original post office. The other address was in Berlin.

Ivy returned them to Lea. "Thank you for sharing these treasures with us."

"I have something else. Another item that was with those." Lea withdrew a small, slim notebook from her pocket. "Ursula wrote some of her thoughts in this. At least, I assume it was her writing. She signed it with the initial *U*."

Shelly spoke up. "How is Ursula related to you and Amelia again?"

"She was my great-grandmother, and she married Amelia's father after her mother died. Ursula was his second wife and quite a bit younger than him." Lea hesitated, her eyes reflecting the magnitude of her emotion. "This is a little diary that she probably kept hidden."

"From her husband?" Shelly asked.

Lea shook her head. "Or from others, I imagine."

The words hung between them, and Ivy's heart went out to her. Amelia had lived a life that Ivy had yet to unravel fully, although the more people she met, the clearer it was. Now, Lea was presenting another missing piece of the puzzle.

Her curiosity aroused, Ivy asked, "What does it say?"

"I'll have to translate," Lea said. "Essentially, she refers to some prominent artists and their work. She hints at Amelia's efforts during WWII to save those pieces from destruction. She calls her by her initial, *A*."

"I wonder why she risked writing it," Ivy said thoughtfully.

"It's written in a sort of shorthand. It took me a while to decipher it. She spoke of Amelia's visits with certain people. I believe they are related to the paintings she brought back. Something about Spain, which I can't figure out. And then, she stopped writing."

Ivy felt a shiver run down her spine. Her mind raced back to a conversation under the Mediterranean sun.

Bennett brushed Ivy's arm with his fingers. "Remember Raquel in Mallorca? She told us about her late grandfather's involvement in a daring rescue of art from the Nazis."

Ivy turned back to Lea. "And you think..." Her voice trailed off, the implications dawning on her.

"If the stories here are true," Lea replied, "Amelia was very entwined in my great-grandfather's work."

"She and Gustav were art collectors, of course," Ivy said. But even as she uttered the words, she understood the magnitude of this new information. *Amelia, her father Hans, and his second wife, Ursula. Their child, Hannah, born during the war.*

Bennett leaned forward. "As for your mother. Was her name Helga?"

"That's right." Lea smiled wistfully. "She died giving birth to me, so I was raised by others. Just as my grandmother was."

"I'm so sorry to hear that," Bennett said.

"Not at all. I lived with my grandmother Hannah, and after she passed away, I became part of another lovely family that knew my family. Still, that made me very independent."

Ivy tried to piece together the family tree in her mind. *If Hannah were Ursula's daughter, Amelia's half-sister, and Lea's grandmother, then Amelia's niece would be Hannah's daughter and Lea's mother: Helga.*

Ivy turned to Bennett. How did he know that? Lea hadn't mentioned her mother's name yet.

The table seemed to shrink inward, the weight of history pressing in on them. Ivy's thoughts spun. Amelia's estate had been a question mark for years, a legacy in limbo waiting for an heir.

Only after the estate had waited for the appropriate period was the beach house listed and sold to Jeremy and the San Francisco house to Viola.

Now Ivy understood why the niece was never located. Helga had died giving birth to Lea. Too much had happened; too many stitches dropped in their pattern of life.

"Ivy, do you understand what this means?" Lea's voice was a mix of hope and trepidation. "I came here because I thought there might be a connection."

Now, everything seemed possible. Ivy's mind raced. The estate, the will, the clause about awaiting an heir—all pointed to Lea now. But why was she here? Was it to claim her inheritance, to stake a claim on the Seabreeze Inn itself?

"Ivy?" Lea pulled her back from the precipice of her thoughts.

"As I told you, my late husband bought this home from

Amelia's estate," Ivy said, choosing her words carefully. "That's all I knew. Until now."

The silence that followed was heavy with unspoken questions. Ivy felt torn, caught between the past and the present, between loyalty to her family and the unfolding drama Lea had brought with her.

Ivy pressed her finger to her throbbing temple. "It's getting late, but I'd like to continue this conversation."

"Of course," Lea said. "I'm just so pleased to be here and to learn more about my great-great aunt. I feel so connected to Amelia, especially after what happened in my room."

"Maybe she feels that way about you, too," Shelly said.

Ivy nudged her under the table. "My sister is tired."

"So am I," Lea said. "I'm still in a different time zone." She shivered a little. "It gets chilly at night here."

"We use heat lamps and firepits for our cool evenings," Bennett said, rising from the table. "Why don't we sit by the firepit on the beach now?"

"I'd like that," Lea said. "This is such a beautiful evening with the waves and the palm trees overhead. It's like a dream for me."

They all rose, and as Ivy strolled toward the Adirondack chairs gathered around the firepit, she asked, "What do you do in Germany that you can take time off to visit?"

Lea hesitated for a moment. "I'm a teacher. I think you would call this a holiday break."

"Spring break," Ivy said, nodding. "What do you teach?"

"I used to teach children, but I've graduated to adults. It's certainly more challenging."

"Sunny is nearly finished with her university degree." Ivy gestured to a chair for Lea. While Bennett turned on the gas flame, she considered how to phrase her next question. "This is such a pleasant surprise to have you here. Why didn't you tell us you were related to Amelia before?"

Lea eased into a low wooden chair near the firepit, which

was flickering to life. The dancing flames illuminated a narrow crease of worry on her forehead. "I didn't want you to think I was out for money or anything else."

Shelly sat next to her. "Then why keep it a secret? You could have told us that when you made the reservation. We would have been more prepared for you."

Lea clasped her hands tightly. "For the longest time, I didn't know much about my family's history before the war. Maybe because of this, I never felt like I fit in. It would have been awkward for me to tell you then, and it is, even now."

Ivy felt sorry for this lovely young woman, though her heart was still torn. "I can understand how that might feel."

"My guardians who looked after me after my grand-mother died were wonderful people," Lea said. "They were hardworking and always encouraged me to learn and follow my dreams."

"It sounds like they inspired you to teach."

"They did," Lea said. "They tried to give me a sense of family, but even they didn't know much. Still, I was aware my great-grandmother had an older sister because my grand-mother told me. I was too young to understand it all, though. My grandmother didn't elaborate on the past, which wasn't uncommon then. In East Berlin, life was difficult. Most had to get on with life and focus on rebuilding. And then the wall came down, so people had to figure out how to integrate with the West."

That made sense to Ivy. Lea would have been very young then.

Shelly spoke up. "Do you have a family of your own?"

"Not yet, but very soon, I hope," Lea replied. "I'm getting married after I return."

Shelly pitched forward with interest blazing in her eyes. "Okay, spill it. We want to hear everything about him. What's his name?"

Lea laughed, and her cheeks turned pink. "Michael, and I

wish you could meet him. As I told Ivy, he's working now, but this trip was very important for me."

Ivy smiled across the dancing flames. "Your last trip alone before you marry?"

"Much more than that. I want to know more about my heritage and ancestry, to touch Amelia's life and see if I could find something of myself in it."

"And have you?" Ivy asked.

"I think so," Lea replied, warming her hands near the fire. "My grandmother shared the same compassion that Amelia had. They both had a huge spirit for living."

Ivy nodded in agreement, thinking about all Amelia had done in her life.

"I want to go into my marriage with the confidence of who I am," Lea continued. "My fiancé has a big personality and a large family. I didn't want to disappear into his life without knowing where I came from and being sure of myself." She blew out a little puff of air. "Now, I am still me, but with a better understanding of my family history—and my purpose."

As the stars twinkled to life, they talked more against the sounds of the waves until Lea began to yawn.

"I'm so sorry," she said. "The time difference is still affecting me. I should go to bed early tonight."

Bennett stood and helped her from the low chair. "Thank you for joining us, Lea. You have a fascinating story. I know we all want to hear more."

"I'll leave that for another day," Lea said with a slight nod. "Good night."

After their guest left, Ivy rested her chin in her hand, feeling slightly overwhelmed. Everyone around the fire was staring at her.

"Wow," Shelly said, slipping her hand into Mitch's. "I'm not sure I followed all that."

Ivy turned to Bennett. "I noticed that you knew the name of Amelia's niece."

"Helga." He nodded as he drummed his fingers. "The property trustee gave us the name in case she or another relative contacted us about the house. It's a name you don't hear often here, so it stuck in my mind."

"I'll contact Imani about this new development tomorrow." Ivy would need legal advice, and while Imani wasn't a real estate attorney, she could point her in the right direction.

Bennett put his arm around her shoulder and brought her close to him. "And I'll put in a call to the trustee."

"I appreciate that." The possibility that Lea might be there not for the art or the gala but for a claim on the house was a thought Ivy couldn't shake. "Didn't Viola say the provision of the will for her San Francisco house was the same as for this house?"

Bennett rubbed his jaw in thought. "She did, but we don't know that for sure."

Ivy rose, hating to leave the warmth of the firepit, but it was growing late. "My turn to wash dishes tonight." At least that would keep her mind occupied.

"And I'll help," Poppy said. She walked toward the table and gathered plates.

Daisy was already asleep in her father's arms, so they all said goodnight to Shelly and Mitch.

Bennett followed Ivy and Poppy into the kitchen with an armload of serving dishes. "Once again, we've discovered more in this ongoing mystery."

"Just when I thought we had finally resolved everything related to this house," Ivy said. "I hate to say this, but it seems Lea was overlooked. I wonder if the trustee tried very hard to contact her."

"I wouldn't know about that, but I thought he seemed diligent." Bennett heaved a sigh. "I know it doesn't seem fair."

When Poppy went outside to fetch the rest of the dishes, Ivy smoothed a hand over Bennett's shoulder. "No, it doesn't. Are we to profit over someone's oversight or mistake?"

Bennett turned from the dishes and swept her into his arms. "Do you realize what you're saying?"

She did, and her heart ached at the thought. "Shelly hated it when I returned the paintings to their owners, even though they were on missing property lists." Still, she would never rest as long as she thought the house should have gone to someone else. Maybe that's why Amelia's spirit was still present, much as she hated to admit that.

"I want to do what's right," Ivy said, biting her lip. "But this time, it would really hurt." She could spend years in litigation with spiraling legal fees or create a solution and move forward.

Bennett kissed her softly. "This is why I love you. Whichever way it goes, we'll sort this out. You always seem to find a solution."

Even if Lea didn't bring up the matter, Ivy knew in her heart she would have to. She would never have peace if she kept quiet about something she knew. Certainly not with Amelia's spirit hovering around the house—if that were true. Why risk a chandelier crashing onto your head or whatever it was that angry spirits did?

As for the outcome, they would adjust. Bennett still had his home on the ridgetop. She rested her head on his chest, imagining what Shelly would say.

Suddenly, all her worries about decorations and her fluffy cupcake of a dress paled compared to what they now faced. She had Jeremy to thank for this mess, yet without his betrayal, she wouldn't have a new life in Summer Beach with a man she loved more than she'd ever thought possible.

Ivy threaded her arms around Bennett's neck and kissed

him. "I'm glad you're here with me," she whispered, her heart aching for him and her family.

"I wouldn't want to be anywhere else," Bennett murmured, finding her lips again. "I love you, sweetheart, and your values and strength. I know this isn't easy."

She stroked his face and smiled, thankful for his understanding. "I love the same about you."

Tomorrow, Ivy would have to break this news to Viola before she and Meredith left San Francisco for Summer Beach. Although she tried to imagine an eventual positive outcome, her chest still tightened at the thought.

If what Lea said was true, Ivy didn't know a way out of this mess, short of a protracted, costly legal battle, which she could lose. Not yet, anyway.

13

*B*ennett leaned on his desk in his office at City Hall, listening to the estate attorney's reply. "I understand the estate has been closed for several years," Bennett said. "However, I would appreciate any information you can give me."

The attorney was brief. The estate was closed, and assets were distributed. He wasn't interested in reopening the case.

Bennett had an idea. "Was the will filed with the state, or was it a private matter?" If it had been filed, he could probably get a copy.

The attorney told him what he needed to know, and Bennett hung up. He'd heard about estates being reopened for unique cases. It was rare, but it happened, and he imagined it could be costly. Viola might fight it, but Ivy might have to compromise. Knowing Ivy, he already knew what she would do. He wondered if there might be a middle-ground solution.

Ironically, on their honeymoon, he and Ivy had talked about what they might do if they didn't live at the inn. At least he still had his home, but Ivy enjoyed her life as an innkeeper, and so did he.

Another thought occurred to him. They could buy

another property in Summer Beach, maybe not as unique as the inn, but one they could make their own. More thoughts bubbled up in his mind. They might build on a vacant lot or find property with a tear-down structure.

Bennett steepled his fingers in thought. Boz in the Planning Department would know all about zoning requirements. Axe Woodson, a local construction contractor, could build whatever they needed. It would be new construction, so Ivy wouldn't have to worry about leaky roofs or extensive renovations. With her track record of running the inn, they could approach a bank for a loan.

Still, these could be expensive options. Not that Bennett meant to ride in on his white horse and solve Ivy's problems, but they were married now. They were a pretty good team, he thought.

Before he went too far down those paths, he would talk to Ivy to see what she had in mind, and if she really stood to lose the inn. If there was one lesson he'd learned, it was to let his extremely capable wife come up with solutions.

His ego didn't like to admit it, but she was often better at creative problem solving at the inn than he was. After all, that was her business, and she knew it like he knew city business.

Just let Wyatt try to do what he'd done for Summer Beach. He quirked his mouth to one side. If that guy won, Bennett would give him a year or two at the most. Appreciating the history of Summer Beach, listening to resident requests, balancing budgets, and planning for the future took an experienced person.

Wyatt didn't have what it took to lead Summer Beach. Yet, he was persuasive with his big ideas. Some people could be swayed by Wyatt's inflammatory words and big promises while he lined his pockets with bribes for dodgy developments.

Bennett hoped Sunny didn't fall for his promises and lies. Ivy still had to speak to her daughter about her choice. He felt a little sorry for Sunny; in his opinion, she was suffering in the growing pains department, but he still had faith in her. Anyone who could stand up to a university dean and present a winning case had more intelligence and determination than many people gave her credit for.

"Sorry to bother you, Mr. Mayor." Nan appeared in the doorway. "There's a reporter from an online news service here. He's asking some mighty peculiar questions. I tried to get rid of him. I think you know who put him up to this."

"You can say Wyatt's name, Nan."

She shook her head, her red curls quivering. "I don't like to."

"Send him in. And feel free to interrupt me if there's an emergency."

Nan grinned. "There just might be." She swept from his office with her head held high.

A few moments later, a young man wearing a T-shirt and a hoodie appeared in his doorway. "I'm Jim Turner. Mayor Dylan?"

Bennett nodded and gestured for him to sit down. "What can I do for you?"

"Mind if I record this?"

"Go ahead."

Jim started with the date and added, "I'm with Mayor Dylan of Summer Beach. There's been an allegation that you've misused city funds and funneled money to support your wife's bed-and-breakfast. What do you have to say to that?"

"It's false. Next question."

"But some think there are receipts."

Bennett knew that was a broad term in use now, but he'd take the literal route. "Only one. I paid for an expense incurred for a city meeting there once."

Jim looked slightly confused. "You mean an actual receipt?"

"For about twenty-five bucks."

"What about supplies for the inn or bills you paid for your

wife's business? Some are calling for an investigation into expenditures."

Bennett ticked off his fingers. "No, and no, and bring it on. We have nothing to hide."

Jim looked crestfallen. "Do you have that receipt?"

"Sure do." Bennett reached into his drawer. He'd had Nan make copies just in case. "It was a reimbursement for refreshments from Java Beach. An electrical contractor was working in the city offices that day, so we went to the inn for our annual planning session. We worked off-site to minimize distractions. Here are both receipts."

Jim looked at them with a sigh. "I guess that's okay. How about any cash payments?"

"None. Unless you count petty cash for stamps. Nan is in charge of that, and she keeps meticulous records that we balance monthly. You're free to ask her about that." Bennett leaned forward. "Why did you come here asking about that?"

Jim punched off his recording device. "I'm here on a tip."

"From Wyatt."

The young reporter shifted in his chair. "Well, I can't reveal my sources."

"I know, but you should be interviewing him. Ask him why he suddenly wants to run for mayor and how long he plans to keep the job if elected."

Jim fidgeted with his fingernails, looking flustered.

"Be careful about taking sides," Bennett said. "You should remain impartial in your reporting."

Nan tapped on the open door. "Mr. Mayor, pardon the interruption, but we have a matter that needs your attention."

Jim quickly rose as if he were relieved. He thanked Bennett and headed toward the front door.

"Well, I never," Nan said with a huff.

"Don't be too hard on him. He's just a kid trying to get a break. Wyatt or one of his supporters sent him here to get dirt on me. Or scare me."

"Ha," Nan said. "They don't know you very well."

After Nan left, Bennett contacted a friend at the county records department and asked if there were any probate documents for Amelia Erickson's estate. He also reached out to the escrow officer who had handled the closing. Someone was bound to have a copy of the will and the court instructions.

For the remainder of the day, Bennett caught up on city business. He met with Boz and a council member, returned a few phone calls, and reviewed the budget. He'd hoped to have information for Ivy by the end of the day.

After that, he had to make some personal calls. Plus, they had a gala to produce and many guests to welcome.

14

*W*ith a strong cup of coffee in hand, Ivy made her way through the old inn, noticing tired details that needed attention before the gala. Yet, furniture oil, flowers, and low lights would have to do.

If all went well, she would refresh interiors after the necessary restoration was complete. Yet, the conversation from last night sprang to mind. It seemed like a bad dream, but she knew it wasn't. She passed a hand over her forehead, thinking about what to do.

Bennett had left for City Hall early. They talked a little this morning, but she had to lead the beach walk for guests, and he needed his run on the beach to blow off stress. Their guests had opted for the morning walk over Shelly's yoga class, so her sister took over the breakfast duties.

Ivy had barely slept, thinking about the possible outcomes. She needed answers, and she could think of only one person who might have immediate access: Viola.

As she entered the library, the morning light filtered through the French doors leading to the veranda. She opened the door to let in the ocean breeze and settled at her desk, the very spot where she imagined Amelia had once worked.

Ivy needed to speak to Viola before she left San Francisco. Viola might have information in her files regarding Amelia's will. The more she learned before reaching out to Imani, the better.

Perched at her desk, Ivy dialed Viola's number, rehearsing her questions. The phone rang once, twice, three times.

"Come on, Viola," she whispered, as if her words could coax the call to connect before the San Francisco philanthropist and her assistant, Meredith, departed for Summer Beach.

"Viola Standish," came the crisp, efficient greeting.

"Hello, Viola. It's Ivy from the Seabreeze Inn." Ivy kept her voice steady, though her hands betrayed her with a slight tremor.

"My dear Ivy. To what do I owe the pleasure?" Viola's voice was warm, but Ivy could hear the rustle of papers and the unmistakable sound of pre-travel chaos in the background.

Ivy imagined Viola's houseman and maid were helping the older woman pack. "I'm sorry to catch you at a busy time, but I'm calling about Amelia's will. There might be a development concerning a potential heir who has appeared on the scene."

"Dear heavens, who might that be?"

Hearing the shock in Viola's voice, Ivy spoke quickly. "A woman arrived at the inn from Germany. She hasn't made any claims yet, but she is asking a lot of questions. I thought you might want to be forewarned."

"Do you think she's who she purports to be? I can't tell you how many Anastasia impersonators surfaced after the Russian Empire debacle. Dreadful business, that was, all around."

"She has some old letters as proof," Ivy said. "What she says seems to fit, so I'm concerned." Lea's identity would have to be confirmed.

There was a pause, and Ivy could picture Viola's poised, grim expression.

"This is quite intriguing," Viola finally said. "Amelia's will did not include a direct heir, but there was a provision about a potential claimant from her father's side. A young niece, as I recall, who had gone missing during the war. That's why the estate was kept open for as long as it was."

Ivy had calculated the years in her mind, and Viola was correct. "Amelia might not have remembered if her niece had been in touch with her. We don't know how long she suffered from Alzheimer's disease."

"As I recall," Viola began, "the will was quite detailed. I understand the probate attorney tried to locate the niece, but the stipulated time eventually ran out. My attorney was quite adamant about confirming that to protect my purchase."

"I'm sure he was. But here we are." Ivy's heart raced. "Do you have any information in your files? Anything about the will or the estate that might reference family from Germany?"

Viola let out a puff of air. "The estate attorney should have retained that information. If the stipulations were met, then I don't see a problem."

Wondering about the legalities, Ivy asked, "Are closed estates ever reopened?"

Another pause, longer this time, before Viola replied, "I recall a similar situation where a lost heiress surfaced, and she was provided for through a revision. So if the niece would have inherited the properties…oh, dear. This is an unfortunate mess. What is legally right and morally right on each side are thorny issues. I will ask my attorney to look into this before we leave."

Ivy welcomed Viola's involvement. "Thank you. This means a great deal to us."

"Amelia's legacy is important to us all." A small commotion erupted in the background. "Pardon the noise, but we're packing now. Meredith has made all the arrangements, and we should arrive in Summer Beach tomorrow."

As the call ended, Ivy leaned back in her chair, her gaze drifting to the expanse of the ocean beyond the veranda and patio. The past was a puzzle, each piece slowly finding its place. She had never expected Lea would bring yet another one to their doorstep.

Whatever Viola unearthed could change everything. Ivy picked up the phone to call Imani, then thought again and put it down. She would wait until Viola came back to her with more information from her attorney. Imani was busy enough running Blossoms, her flower stand on Main Street near the beach.

For now, all Ivy could do was wait and hope that the legacy of Amelia Erickson would serve to unify those who cared about her rather than divide them.

She took her empty coffee cup into the kitchen for a refill. Sunny was seated at the kitchen table, surrounded by textbooks and papers, her laptop open. Her daughter frowned and shifted position as sunlight streamed through the windows.

"Hi, sweetheart. How's the paper going?" Ivy crossed to a large thermal urn Shelly had brought in from the breakfast spread for guests. She placed her cup under the nozzle and flipped the dispenser lever.

"I should have started sooner." Sunny twisted her lips to one side, reminding Ivy of Shelly.

"I'm proud of you for sticking with it. Graduation is just around the corner. Soon you'll be free of your studies. Want some coffee?"

Sunny nodded, a tired but genuine smile crossing her face. "Yeah, thanks, Mom. It's been a marathon, but I'm getting there."

"I know you are. And I have every faith you'll make it

through this just fine." Ivy opened the door to Gertie and brought out the cream.

Sunny stretched, wound her strawberry blond hair into a bun, and stuck a pencil through it. "You can join me."

Ivy smiled at the invitation. "I thought you might be avoiding me."

"I can spare a few minutes." Sunny raised a shoulder in a self-conscious shrug. "Wyatt told me about meeting Mitch and Bennett at Java Beach. I figure you have something to say about that."

"And what did he have to say?"

"He said Mitch is kind of cool, but Bennett is a control freak nutcase worried about his stepdaughter dating an older man."

Ivy chuckled as she sat across from Sunny, the wooden chair creaking slightly. "So, did you agree with him about Bennett?"

"What? No way. He might be a lot of things, but not that." She grinned. "Good things. As far as stepdads go, Bennett's cool."

Ivy was glad to hear how she felt about Bennett. She poured the cream and slid a cup across the table to Sunny. "There's probably another reason Wyatt said that."

Sunny raised her eyebrows with curiosity. "What?"

"Did you know Wyatt plans to run against Bennett for mayor?"

The reaction was immediate. Surprise flickered across Sunny's features, her eyes widening. "Run for mayor? He didn't mention that."

Ivy reached across the table, taking her daughter's hands. "Sweetheart, I'm worried. Wyatt's a lot older, and while age is just a number, I'm concerned he might have ulterior motives. Like using you to get under Bennett's skin."

Sunny pulled her hands back, a mix of defiance and

confusion playing across her face. "Wyatt and I are on the same wavelength. He's not like that."

"The news is all over town. Wyatt hasn't officially filed, but he's been spreading rumors about Bennett and a misuse of city funds that involves the inn. Which is entirely untrue."

Sunny shifted in her chair, looking uncomfortable with this news. "Are you sure?"

"Ask Mitch. He can confirm that."

"I will," Sunny said, crossing her arms.

Ivy pressed gently, her gaze never leaving her daughter's. "Doesn't it seem odd that he hasn't mentioned such a significant decision to you? After all, running for mayor is no small thing."

Sunny's confident façade began to crumble. "Why wouldn't he tell me? I've been totally open with him."

Ivy watched as her daughter grappled with this new information, her resistance giving way. "Is he just using me?" Sunny's voice broke, the hurt evident.

"Some men do that, I'm afraid." Ivy moved to her daughter's side, wrapping an arm around her shoulders.

Sunny leaned into her embrace. "I guess I should have told you sooner. I didn't think you'd approve of his age."

"Sometimes age doesn't matter, sometimes it does. It depends on the couple. But it can be a red flag. Many older men use young women to boost their ego."

Ivy knew an age difference was irrelevant when people truly loved each other. She doubted Sunny and Wyatt were that serious. She'd also seen Jeremy's forty-something friends divorce and marry twenty-somethings. They were often shopping for the third wife after a few short years. Jeremy was probably on the same path when he died.

Sunny scrubbed her face and sighed. "What a jerk. I messed up again, didn't I?"

Ivy smoothed Sunny's hair, her heart aching for her daughter. "It's okay. We all want to believe the best in people.

You're far from the first to be taken advantage of—and I speak from experience."

Ivy hesitated, but now that they were here, she needed to spill everything. "Now, about Poppy's boyfriend. Grant. Or Arlo. Whatever he's calling himself now."

Sunny's eyebrows rose. "Oh, my gosh, Poppy just told me what happened. She said Aunt Shelly used to date him in New York. Is that true?"

Ivy nodded. "Shelly says he's a real narcissist. They tend to love bomb women in the beginning, but then they want to control you, and everything is all about them. It didn't end well for Shelly."

"That's what Poppy said." A frown creased Sunny's forehead. "Arlo was pressuring her to move to L.A. so they could be together. Besides, his having dated Aunt Shelly is too weird, so she broke up with him."

Ivy wasn't worried about Poppy; she was smart, but Ivy would still check in with her again to see how she was doing.

Sunny pressed her lips into a thin line of anger. "I won't listen to anyone trash talk Bennett. I can't believe Wyatt thought I wouldn't find out. Or that I wouldn't care. And he wasted my time when I should have been working on this paper." She threw her arms around Ivy.

Ivy hugged her, hoping Sunny would make the right decision about Wyatt. Maybe she was dating him because he reminded her of her father. Ivy could understand that; Jeremy's death had been hard on Sunny. "Let me know if you need help—on anything."

Sunny wiped angry tears from her eyes with the heels of her palms. "I'll have to get this paper done before the gala. It's due by five in the afternoon the day before."

"Then you'll be able to celebrate and enjoy yourself." Ivy didn't want to say it might be their last party in the house.

15

The inn buzzed with energy and was a flurry of activity, its corridors echoing with the sounds of last-minute preparations. Guests for the gala were arriving regularly now, with many more expected, but Ivy was ready for them. Especially Viola and Meredith, their VIP guests.

Poppy was in the foyer, and Shelly was finishing the exterior decorations. They were all dressed for the occasion; Ivy wore a floral blouse and taupe slacks that looked nice but were comfortable enough to move in.

Ivy moved through the hallway with purpose, her mind filled with a list of tasks. The gala was not only to restore the inn but also to celebrate the legacy of Amelia Erickson, whose spirit sometimes seemed to permeate the air they breathed, not counting what Lea thought she saw.

Poppy had assembled many old artifacts and photos in the library, staging items there before she placed them around the inn to showcase its historical importance.

After speaking with Viola yesterday, Ivy had gone through the old address book they had found in the ballroom. In it, she located the address matching the one on the letters Lea had brought with her. The entry was under the German word for father.

Lea's story was likely true, yet she hadn't brought up the inheritance issue. Was it possible she was unaware, or was she waiting until after the gala to reveal her intentions?

Poppy called to her from the front desk. "There is a limousine pulling to the curb. Is that Viola and Meredith?"

"It certainly is," Ivy replied, peering out. "Viola called a few minutes ago to confirm directions." She and Poppy went outside to greet their benefactor and her niece.

"Good afternoon, and welcome," Ivy said. "How was your flight and the drive here?"

"Very comfortable," Viola replied. "We traveled with my friend Betsy, who brought her plane."

"That's a much nicer way to travel," Ivy said. "We have your rooms ready. Viola, you'll be in Amelia's former suite. Meredith, you'll be in the suite next to hers."

Viola leaned in and spoke softly. "Once we're in the room, we can speak, dear. I have an update for you, although it's not much, mind you."

Ivy hoped it was good news but was still torn over the situation. She carried Viola's suitcase upstairs while Poppy managed Meredith's luggage. Their two guests would enjoy the best views of the patio, the pool, and the ocean beyond.

Lea was staying in another suite down the hall, which made Ivy a little nervous.

Once inside the room, Viola produced a jewelry box studded with semi-precious stones that cradled the Victorian diamond necklace. Touching it with reverence, she said, "This exquisite piece is the highlight of the auction. I'm thrilled that it's going toward a good cause here."

Ivy admired the necklace, its diamonds catching the fading light. "It's beautiful."

"Amelia's spirit will certainly be looking down on us here,"

Viola said. "Before I left home, I had chatted with dear Gustav in the library."

"Aunt Viola," Meredith said, touching her aunt's sleeve with mild admonishment. "Don't say things like that to scare people."

Ivy and Poppy exchanged a glance. Ivy hoped that whatever had frightened Lea wouldn't disturb the current guests in that room.

"I'm not scared," Poppy said, smiling. "Maybe Amelia will float off to San Francisco, where her husband was last seen."

"They'll have a lot more privacy there," Ivy added. Then, considering the number of guests at the inn, she said, "Let's keep the necklace safe."

"Won't it be in my room?" Viola asked. "We know everyone attending the event."

"I have an idea that's even more secure," Ivy said. "I'll show you a special spot we discovered in the dressing area."

The mirrored dressing room was outfitted with a chandelier and an upholstered vintage chaise and tuffet. Ivy made her way to the last closet. Setting aside a carved screen, she then pressed against the rear panel. It gave way and opened into a small room.

Behind her, Viola and Meredith gasped.

For years, until Ivy and Shelly discovered this room, vintage clothes had hung from a clothes rack. A sewing kit still sat beside it.

Ivy gestured to the room. "This was part of a passageway to the attic rooms where Amelia concealed people entering the country who had no other means of entry due to the war. Doctors, scientists, artists, all of whom were simply eager for a chance to share their knowledge and expertise and live their lives in peace. One Christmas, we discovered one of our guests had grandparents who passed through here. Nick has contributed deep knowledge to the medical community."

"The Ericksons took a lot of risks and helped many people in their time," Viola said with a nod. She and Meredith followed Ivy into the small room, exclaiming over the items still there.

Poppy placed the jewelry box on the antique desk. "We think they shared Amelia's bathroom and used this area to dress."

"This is the most secure place at the inn," Ivy added. "Not that we have anything to worry about."

"Of course, I trust your judgment," Viola said.

"We should showcase some of these items in the vintage display in the parlor," Poppy said, admiring the vintage clothing.

"Some of these garments likely belonged to other people," Ivy said. "We can display Amelia's wedding dress, the notebook of her dress designs with fabric, and other items we found here."

"We're also using the silver serving pieces and stemware stored in the house," Poppy said. "It took us forever to polish everything, but it's gorgeous. Ivy said you have lovely serving items in San Francisco, too."

"We do," Viola said, smiling at Poppy. "The Ericksons entertained on a lavish, formal level there. It's museum quality, and that's what the home will become after I pass on—a museum and community meeting place for nonprofits."

"I know the gala is going to be lovely," Meredith said as they all stepped from the hidden room back into the suite. "Do you need any help? I could lend a hand while Viola visits with her friend Betsy."

Ivy remembered she had met Meredith in the garden of Amelia's former home in San Francisco. "You're welcome to spend time with us, and Shelly is eager to share her garden with you."

Viola pressed a hand to Ivy's shoulder. "I also wanted to

tell you about my conversation with my attorney regarding the estate."

Ivy's chest tightened. "Please, let's sit," she said, gesturing to an antique table and chairs by the window.

With an expression of concern, Viola folded her hands on the table. "My lawyer reviewed the will and the trust it created. She believes the trustee handled the matter appropriately with the care entrusted to him. However, that will not prevent someone from making a claim if they wish."

Ivy listened intently, trying to consider the situation from Lea's perspective. "I can't imagine being the heir to such properties and losing them simply because you couldn't be located. Lea's mother, Helga, was the heir—she was Amelia's niece—and she died giving birth to Lea. She also lived in East Berlin, so communication was likely difficult before the Berlin Wall was demolished. Poor Lea didn't stand a chance to inherit what should have been her mother's property."

Viola and Meredith exchanged a glance. "Perhaps there are other ways of compensating Lea for that unfortunate circumstance. I'm not saying I have an answer right now, but we can address it soon."

"Thank you," Ivy said, feeling a little relieved. "I know that would make Lea very happy. You should have seen the awe in her face when she arrived here. Simply being where her ancestor lived made her so happy. She's to be married soon and wanted to explore her roots before then. She seems like a lovely person."

"If she is indeed who she says she is," Viola said before nodding thoughtfully. "If so, I don't bear her any ill will, and I am confident that we can sort this out. Let's enjoy the gala and let the legal team wrestle with this. I'm sure you have plenty on your mind as it is."

They spoke a little more about the situation, and Ivy promised to introduce Lea to them later.

With Viola and Meredith settled in their rooms, Ivy found

Shelly outside, testing the twinkly fairy lights tucked around the patio.

"Do you think I used enough lights?" Shelly asked, assessing her work. "I want the lights to reflect the stars and cast soft light around the garden and patio areas."

"It's going to be breathtaking," Ivy replied. "What else do you need to do?"

"Tomorrow, the flowers will arrive," Shelly said. "Or rather, I'll cart them back. I'll be up at four in the morning to make that drive."

"Are you taking Daisy with you, or would you like to leave her here?"

"Mitch will take time off with her. He has a good team to cover for him at Java Beach." Shelly brightened. "Imani wants to come with me. She plans to buy some special inventory for Blossoms."

"Tell her hello for me." Ivy hadn't had time to call Imani about Lea. "I can hardly wait to see what you do with everything,"

Shelly smiled with confidence. "Trust me, it will be spectacular."

Ivy had no doubt. She told Shelly that Viola and Meredith had arrived and were looking forward to meeting her. "They want to take us all out for dinner this evening. Viola insisted, so I made a reservation at Beaches. Do you think you can make it with Daisy?"

"I'll ask Darla. She loves babysitting Daisy."

"You're lucky to have her."

Shelly shook her head in amazement. "Who would have thought that when we first arrived? We've come a long way, Ives."

Ivy embraced her. "Sure have, Shells."

After Ivy left her sister, she hurried inside, trying to forget about the estate and Lea's potential claim out of her mind, as

Viola suggested, so she could enjoy the weekend. The gala would be a once-in-a-lifetime event.

This weekend, she had to focus on welcoming guests and raising funds for the preservation of the old house, regardless of what the future might hold.

When Ivy returned to the front with Poppy, the door opened, and Rowan Zachary stepped inside, lowering his dark sunglasses as he surveyed the room. He wore a silk ascot paired with a white jacket and taupe trousers. The actor's arrival was as grand as any entrance he'd made in decades on the silver screen.

"Rowan, welcome back," Ivy said, greeting him with genuine fondness and a little trepidation.

"Ivy, darling. My favorite life-saving hostess." He gave her a huge hug.

Rowan had slipped into the pool and nearly drowned. As a one-time lifeguard, Ivy dove in to rescue him. Smiling, Ivy said, "Shall I wear my swimsuit under my evening dress and have the fire department on standby?"

Rowan threw back his head, roaring with laughter. "You have my word, darling—no impromptu pool dives or indoor pyrotechnics."

Ivy lifted an eyebrow. "That was a dive?"

He pressed a finger to his lips. "Inadvertently, shall we say? That makes for a better story, and life is all about the stories we tell. Now, as I recall, you serve a delicious Sea Breeze cocktail here, don't you?"

"That's Shelly's specialty," Ivy replied. "If you promise to keep your distance from the edge of the pool, I'll ask her to make one for you."

"Sounds like I'm just in time." Shelly sauntered in, and Rowan kissed her hand. "I'll escort you to your room. We've taken precautions this time—no open flames allowed around you." Shelly led him away with a playful wag of her finger.

Poppy had volunteered to keep a close eye on Rowan

throughout the gala. That man attracted mishaps like starlets. He had a penchant for spectacle and fire; his flaming Christmas cocktail nearly caught the ballroom on fire. Rowan Zachary couldn't be trusted.

That was all Ivy needed at the gala. This event must go off without a hitch.

16

"Take the beach route until you see the marina," Ivy told a pair of guests. "It's an easy walk, and you can have lunch afterward in the village." As they left, Poppy greeted another guest, and the phone rang.

Ivy picked it up. "It's a sunny day at the Seabreeze Inn. How may I help you? Oh, yes, thank you for calling back. Do you have time this afternoon for one of our guests at the spa?"

The day before the benefit gala was one of the busiest Ivy could recall at the Seabreeze Inn. She had been checking in guests all day while Poppy saw them to their rooms and handled countless requests. Shelly had left early in the morning with Imani to pick up fresh flowers.

After making the reservation for Meredith, Ivy hung up. The phone rang again, and she answered. "Yes, the GPS directions are correct," she replied to the caller. "It might look like it's taking you directly into the ocean, but that's because the inn is the last property by the beach. You can't miss it, I promise. See you soon."

Ivy ticked off her mental list. Rooms, decorations, flowers, menu—almost everything was ready. For the gala dinner, only the finest that Summer Beach had to offer would do for Viola.

Chef Marguerite, the experienced proprietor at Beaches, the romantic fine dining restaurant at the water's edge, was thankfully in charge. The restaurant's catering group would produce and serve the appetizers, dinner, and dessert.

Viola and Meredith took the family to Beaches last night, and Marguerite assured Ivy they were ready for the gala catering. That was a relief, and Ivy looked forward to it.

Sunny breezed into the entryway, looking ecstatic. "Mom, I finished. I just turned in my paper. Early, too. Thanks for the encouragement." Grinning, she held her arms wide.

Ivy embraced her daughter. "That's wonderful, sweetheart. See? I knew you could do it."

"Do you need any help?" Sunny glanced around at guests exploring and examining the architectural elements. "Looks like we have a full house."

"More guests will arrive soon." Ivy was expecting several of Viola's VIP friends. Two SUVs had just pulled to the front walkway.

"Need some help?" Sunny asked.

"Sure do," Ivy replied. "Poppy planned to set up a historical display in the parlor, but she hasn't had the time. She's getting a guest settled, and it looks like we have a new party arriving right now."

"I could do that." Sunny glanced around. "I saw some historical displays that you used for the art show a while back. Mind if I use those, too?"

Ivy was relieved that Sunny was taking the initiative. "Whatever you want to do. Poppy can fill you in on what she planned. The two of you can work together on that."

Sunny looked down at her torn jeans. "I'll change and make a sandwich. Do you want anything?"

"I'm starving," Poppy said, coming down the stairs toward her cousin. "We haven't had time for a break."

"I can fill in," Sunny said. "I'll make extra sandwiches and leave them in the kitchen for you."

"You have no idea how glad we are to hear that." Ivy was pleased that Sunny was pitching in without being asked. She motioned toward Poppy. "You go first."

"I'll be back in ten," Sunny said to Poppy. "I need to change clothes first."

Just then, Megan Calloway arrived, her short blond hair stylishly tousled. "Hi, everyone. I'm here to meet Viola. She said she'll meet me downstairs."

"Feel free to wait in the parlor," Ivy said. From the corner of her eye, she saw Lea coming down the stairs carrying her purse. Ivy could introduce everyone at once. "Poppy, can you handle the new guests for a few minutes?"

"Sure," Poppy replied. "Take your time. Sunny will be back soon."

Ivy joined Megan in the parlor. "I'll introduce you to one of our new guests that I know you'll want to talk to. She's a descendant of Amelia's." Briefly, Ivy filled her in. "Here's Lea now."

Megan's eyes lit with anticipation. "Wow, I'll bet she has an interesting story to share."

"She sure does," Ivy said, trying to keep the wistfulness from her voice.

What do we really own in this lifetime anyway? she thought. Maybe these past few years were the extent of her contribution here. If so, did something else await her, like that proverbial pony in the haystack? Although it was an emotional stretch, she was trying to accept what might unfold.

Ivy pulled back her shoulders. For now, she resolved to make this gala one to rival those the Ericksons once held in this grand old beach house—and she would enjoy every moment of it.

Even if she would be dressed as a pink frosted cupcake.

When Lea cleared the last step of the staircase, Ivy said, "I have someone I'd love for you to meet. Megan Calloway. She is working on a documentary about Amelia Erickson's life."

"How interesting," Lea said, turning toward Megan.

Ivy walked with her. "Perhaps you could add what you know about her life in Europe before she and Gustav arrived in the States."

"What exciting, important work," Lea said, greeting Megan. "I don't have much information either. What are you looking for?"

"Anything you could share would be wonderful," Megan replied. "Viola Standish will help me fill in the San Francisco part of her life."

Lea opened her purse. "I have a few letters and a little notebook with me."

While they talked, Ivy excused herself to get the address book from the library.

When she returned, she showed it to them. "We found this recently. The address on those letters is in here. Amelia filed it under *father*."

Megan looked at the faded postmark on the letters and raised her brow. "These are certainly a confirmation. Your connection to Amelia is fascinating."

"I hope Lea's knowledge can enrich your film project," Ivy added.

"I think I'm the only living relative left," Lea said. "I was eager to find out where and how she had lived." She hesitated, then told Megan about her family history.

"I'm so sorry to hear that." Megan glanced at Ivy with an apologetic expression, too. Ivy nodded at her to continue. "Were you ever contacted about her estate?"

Lea shook her head. "She died before I was born."

"What about your mother or grandmother?"

"I'm not sure I follow what you mean," Lea replied. She seemed genuinely perplexed about the question.

"As I understand, and correct me if I'm wrong, Ivy," Megan said with another glance at Ivy. "The estate was held open, waiting for her niece to be located. Only when she was assumed dead was the estate settled."

Ivy swallowed against the lump in her throat. Megan was doing her job, and this would come out soon enough.

Megan touched Lea's hand. "Did you ever hear about that?"

Before Lea could answer, Ivy heard someone behind her. She turned to see Viola, who wore a navy-blue dress with pearls. Beside her was Meredith, dressed in athleisure wear for her spa visit. They must have overheard everything.

"Oh, Viola," Ivy exclaimed, quickly remembering her manners in front of the older woman. "Mrs. Standish, I would like to introduce Lea, our guest from Berlin. Amelia Erickson was her great-grandmother's older half-sister. And this is Megan, the documentary filmmaker I told you about." She also introduced Meredith.

"I am pleased to make your acquaintance," Viola said, her manner at once imperious yet warm. "And please call me Viola. We're practically family."

After greeting everyone, Meredith excused herself for her spa appointment. "I'll be back in plenty of time for dinner, Aunt Viola."

"Enjoy yourself," Viola said. She settled back with her new acquaintances.

Megan, with her natural curiosity, quickly engaged Viola in conversation. She opened the vintage photo album on the table for Viola, and the woman began to talk and review the vintage photographs.

Ivy noted Lea's cautious openness. She was accommodating, yet Ivy sensed a hesitance, perhaps due to what Megan said—or had Lea known all along?

Ivy returned to the front desk to take a call. The front door opened to another new arrival, and Poppy welcomed them and directed them to their rooms. Ivy helped the next couple, eager to see the ballroom they'd read about.

"It's this way," she said, guiding them into the other room. "We also have a preview of the silent auction items set up here. Bidding begins tomorrow."

Upon returning to the front, Ivy checked on the group in the parlor again.

"Why, look at this photo," Viola said. "It's Amelia, and she's wearing a necklace that looks just like the one we're auctioning."

Lea exclaimed and leaned in over the photograph, transfixed. "I would love to have a copy of this one."

"We can arrange that," Ivy said.

Lea ran her fingers along the edge of the old album. "Would it be possible to have a copy of every photograph in here? I would be happy to pay for the reproduction."

"Of course," Ivy said, trying not to think that Lea might have a use for the photos beyond the personal. She blinked away the thought. It was more difficult than she'd imagined not to think about what they might be facing. "You should have photos of your ancestor."

"I don't have any," Lea said with a small smile. "Where I came from has always been a mystery to me. My guardians encouraged me to look ahead, not back, which was good advice at the time. But now, I want to know more."

Ivy's heart went out to her. She could only imagine how Lea might have grown up, orphaned at such a young age. Ivy understood why she would want mementos of her relative. She squashed the speck of doubt that rose in her chest.

Megan noticed other guests walking around. Some were talking about the auction. She turned back to Viola. "I would love to see Amelia's Victorian necklace before the live auction to get an accurate description and photographs. Would that be possible?"

"Of course," Viola replied. "You're welcome to come to my suite later." She cast a look at the stairs.

"I can retrieve it for you as soon as Poppy returns," Ivy

offered, in case Viola might have difficulty entering the hidden room or navigating the stairs. She recalled seeing an elevator in Viola's home.

"That's very kind of you," Viola said. "Later will be fine. We have quite a bit to talk about first. Do you have tea, by the way?"

"I'll have Poppy or Sunny bring a tea tray," Ivy replied.

Megan checked her notes. "How much do you think that piece might bring?"

Ivy wondered that, too. "We hope it brings enough for basic renovations of the inn so it can serve the community." More than ever, she felt the weight of the inn's legacy.

"I'm dying to know who is planning to bid on it," Megan said. "Any ideas?"

Seeming as interested in that as Megan, Lea looked at Viola.

With a slight smile, Viola shrugged. "People are talking, but I can't comment."

Ivy watched for some sign, but Viola wasn't giving any hints. Now, the necklace was more than just an item for auction; it was a legacy, a connection to a family lineage that had, until now, seemed settled. Despite all that had transpired, the past still held sway over the present.

The live auction of the necklace, along with Carol Reston's donation and performance, would be the highlights of the evening. Still, Ivy's mind was elsewhere, weaving through the maze of possibilities that Lea's presence had unveiled.

Sunny bounced back into the foyer just as Poppy returned to the reception desk. The two cousins whispered about something that looked serious, yet when the front door opened, they smiled and greeted the guests.

Ivy watched, wondering what was going on and if it had to do with Grant and Wyatt. She hoped that pair was in the past.

The arrival of more guests did little to quell Ivy's inner turmoil. As Sunny and Poppy welcomed more of Viola's friends, Ivy considered each one. They were here to support the inn and partake in the honor and celebration of Amelia's life, but among them, who might lay claim to the necklace, her glittering legacy?

Ivy checked her watch. She wondered where Shelly and Imani might be and thought they would have returned by now. Once they arrived, there would be plenty to do.

She could call Shelly but didn't want to disturb her while driving. The highway from Los Angeles was heavily traveled and could be treacherous. They had left so early this morning she hoped they were okay to drive. Although Ivy was worried, she would give them a little longer.

17

*I*vy approached Sunny and Poppy at the front desk. "Have all the new guests checked in today?"

Poppy tapped a few keys on the computer. "Looks like we just checked in the last person. So far, they're all happy."

"Let's try to keep it that way," Ivy said. Just then, her phone buzzed in her pocket, and she pulled it out with relief. "Finally, it's Shelly. She and Imani are pulling into the car court and need help unloading the flowers."

They made their way toward the rear of the house. On the way out, Poppy snagged half a sandwich in the kitchen, and they all trooped outside. Shelly's old Jeep brimmed with flowers. Imani pulled up behind her, and her SUV was also full.

The two women opened their doors, and sweet aromas spilled from their vehicles.

"Wow, that's intoxicating," Ivy exclaimed, marveling at the buckets of roses and lilies that Shelly had tied down with bungee cords for the return trip.

"Check out the assortment of tropical flowers," Shelly said, her face flushed with excitement. "Red ginger, plumeria, and pikake blossoms. Everything we could want, and then some."

In her bright tie-dyed knit sundress and colorful bangles, Imani matched the floral rainbow riot of colors. "We had a great time. It's so much fun to go to the Flower Market with Shelly."

"Everything in my car goes inside, and Imani will show you what stays here with us." Before Shelly left, she had prepared the kitchen and butler's pantry.

Poppy wolfed down her sandwich, and everyone pitched in to unload the cars, keeping an eye on the front desk as they shuttled back and forth. Guests at the pool watched them with interest.

Before Shelly left, she had created an astounding arrangement for the foyer and placed roses in the guest rooms. Her sister had really outdone herself. Ivy looked forward to the finished centerpieces and other arrangements.

She scooped up a bundle of hydrangeas. "You're such a pro, Shells."

"I felt like I was back in my old New York groove," Shelly said happily.

"Oh, look at these," Sunny said, admiring a bunch of long-stemmed, turquoise-and-white speckled roses and others tipped with deep shades of color. "I've never seen anything like these. Do they grow like that?"

"Those are from Ecuador," Shelly replied. "The growers wrap them and tend them by hand. Careful with them."

"You should have heard her bargaining with the flower vendors," Imani said. "I thought one guy was going to call the police."

"That's why I brought my lawyer with me," Shelly said, winking back at her. "To bail me out."

Flowers, Ivy mused, lifted everyone's spirits. Despite her worries, the heady aromas and bright jumble of colors made her smile and eased the tension in her shoulders. It was easy to understand why Shelly loved being outside in the garden more than anywhere else.

After unloading the vehicles, they gathered in the kitchen, and Shelly set up an assembly line. She quickly showed each person what to do. "You guys do the prep work, and Imani and I are in charge of the final assembly."

"This is nature therapy," Ivy said, grinning at Shelly, who was elbow-deep in dahlias and peonies.

"Sure is." After trimming a stem, Shelly glanced up, her eyes bright. "If I could bottle this feeling, I'd be a billionaire. Speaking of therapy, who wants a Sea Breeze? I've been up since before sunrise, so it's way past cocktail hour for me."

"I'll mix them," Poppy said.

Shelly winked at her. "I planned for this. Check out Gertie."

Poppy opened the refrigerator and brought out a pitcher of pink grapefruit and cranberry juice. She placed it on the counter with a stack of glasses and a bottle of vodka.

Shelly motioned to the setup. "Virgin or fully loaded, ladies. Help yourselves."

With five of them working together, chatter and laughter rose in the kitchen.

Gilda poked her head into the doorway with Pixie tucked under her arms. "We just returned from our shift at Thrifty Threads and heard the commotion back here." She gazed around the kitchen. "This is all so exciting. It looks like a flower explosion, and the scent is heavenly. Want me to watch the front door for you?"

"That would be wonderful, thanks," Ivy replied. "And please let me know if Viola asks for me. There's something I promised to do for her when she's ready. She's in the parlor with Megan. I left them deep in conversation."

Gilda had lived there almost as long as they had, and she was practically part of the family. She joined them for supper on occasion and filled in from time to time.

"Hey, you." Imani paused to hug Gilda. "I sure miss living here and seeing Pixie prance around like she owns the place. Won't you come over to my new house for lunch soon? She's welcome, too."

"I'd love that," Gilda replied.

"I'll call you," Imani said, placing flowers in a small vase. "And here, these are for your room."

Ivy and Shelly traded a smile. People who met at the inn often formed friendships and kept in touch. That was part of the magic of this place—and Summer Beach.

Sunny waved a stalk of greenery. "I have an announcement you'll all want to hear."

The chatter faded as she took a deep breath. "After I finished my paper, I called Wyatt and broke up."

Holding up a rose, Shelly paused in mid-arrangement. "Oh, Sunny, I'm sorry," she said, although she exchanged a look of relief with Ivy.

Sunny pursed her lips. "You're not sorry at all, Aunt Shelly. And actually, neither am I. He lied to me about running against Bennett. How messed up is that? My *stepfather*. What was Wyatt thinking?"

"He wasn't thinking about you," Shelly said.

Poppy hugged her. "You know, it's hard to date someone who thinks he's prettier than you. Plus, the age gap. Twenty years meant Arlo was listening to old music all the time. He'd never heard of half my music. Can you believe he actually said, 'Taylor who?'"

Shelly hit her forehead with the palm of her hand. "Duh, Swift. Dude! How dense."

Ivy chuckled at the conversation. Bennett would be pleased to hear this, too.

"They weren't worth the fancy dinners and dancing," Poppy said.

Shelly snapped a stem. "Guys like that are only into you for themselves. After marrying Mitch, I can't believe the guys I went out with. It's like I was shopping in the Priceless Jerks department or had a season pass to the Narcissist Fair. I hope we've seen the last of them."

"I couldn't agree more," Ivy said. Yet, she was still concerned about Bennett. She'd never seen him as angry as he'd been with Wyatt over Sunny. He was protecting her child for her.

"Guys like him will meet their match someday," Imani said, selecting several long-stemmed roses. "Some savvy woman will take advantage of their weakness, or they'll die lonely, conceited old fools. You all know what I'm talking about."

They all laughed, and Ivy reached across the table, squeezing Sunny's hand. There was strength in her daughter, a resilience that made Ivy's heart swell with pride.

"You're better off without him, honey," Ivy said. "Honesty is the cornerstone of...well, of everything. Are you okay?"

Sunny gave her a shy grin. "Another guy from class I like asked me out, so I'm completely okay, Mom."

"Cheers to that," Shelly said, raising her glass. "Woo-hoo, are we having fun yet?"

"You bet we are." Ivy raised a glass, too, although she was carefully sipping. They still needed to tend to guests.

As they were working, Megan burst into the kitchen with excitement. She glanced around the bustling room filled with flowers and sisterly banter. "Oh, my goodness. These flower arrangements are stunning."

"It's what I do," Shelly said.

"I have to get all of this on film," Megan said. "Speaking of which, I had an idea. I can set up the old film footage of Amelia on the lower level as we did before."

"Guests would love that," Ivy said while Poppy nodded.

"Or would you rather have it in the music room?" Megan asked. "Think about it; we don't have to decide now."

"It's up to Poppy and Sunny. They're in charge of the historical task."

"After you're through in the parlor," Sunny said to Megan, "we'll set up the vintage display there."

"I'll let you know when we're through." Megan shifted back to Ivy. "Viola would love to see Amelia's necklace now. She's eager for us to see it before the event."

Ivy nodded, wiping her hands on a dishtowel. "Of course. I'll retrieve it for you."

Climbing the rear stairs to Viola's suite, Ivy thought about the delicate filigree and the cascade of diamonds and how the necklace would sparkle under the ballroom chandeliers—just as it had decades ago when Amelia wore it. There was a certain poetic balance in that.

Ivy used her master key to open Viola's guest room and walked into the closet. A swift push of the rear panel opened to the hidden room behind it.

The light spilling into the room was dim. Ivy couldn't see the jewelry box, so she flicked on her phone's light. But there was...nothing. She blinked in horror. The spot where she'd left it was empty.

Instantly, her heart plummeted.

"Where can it be?" she cried, swinging the light around the room.

The jewelry box with the priceless necklace was gone. A cold sweat broke out on her forehead.

She rushed back into the room, looking everywhere and hoping that Viola had moved it. But it was useless. Panic took hold as she tore down the rear staircase, her mind racing with different scenarios.

Bursting into the kitchen, she confronted her family. "Has anyone seen the necklace?" she asked, her voice laced with urgency. "It's not in the secret room."

They all exchanged wide-eyed looks, shaking their heads

in disbelief. The disappearance quickly stamped out the joy in the room.

Ivy's mind spun with scenarios of what might have happened to it. Viola would be beyond furious. Without the necklace, the centerpiece of their auction, the much-needed funds for the inn's restoration were also gone.

"Who else knew it was there?" Shelly asked.

"Meredith," Ivy replied. "But she's staying in another room."

"And she's been at the day spa," Poppy added.

"It couldn't have been her, then," Ivy said, her pulse roaring in her ears.

"Pixie wouldn't have—" Shelly stopped, and they all stared at each other. "There's no way even that kleptomaniac Chihuahua could have unlocked the room and opened that panel. I'll ask Gilda anyway."

Then it struck Ivy, and she pressed her fingers to her temples. "Wait a minute…"

A memory flooded back to her. She had taken Lea on a tour of the house, and while she hadn't shown her the hidden room, she had mentioned its existence. A horrible sinking feeling took root in her stomach.

"I told Lea about the secret room."

Shelly's eyes widened. "What?"

"But Lea was with us," Megan said. "Well, most of the time."

Ivy drew her hands over her face. Could Lea have excused herself, picked the lock, and snatched the bejeweled box? The thought made her ill.

She didn't want to cast aspersions, especially on the only remaining relative of Amelia.

But the timing, the opportunity, and the desire to have something of Amelia's were too coincidental. Was this Lea's revenge for being overlooked and denied her inheritance?

"Seems pretty clear what happened," Shelly said, stripping

lower leaves from tuberose with a vengeance. "I say we search her and her room."

"We can't do that." Ivy reached for the phone. "But I can call Chief Clarkson. If he's discreet, maybe he can investigate without causing a scene and find the necklace before anyone knows it's gone."

Megan looked doubtful. "You mean, besides Viola?

"Oh, my gosh. We have to tell her." Ivy's head felt like it was about to explode.

Shelly put a hand on Ivy's shoulder, her eyes full of concern. "When Chief Clarkson gets here, he can tell her with you. We'll figure this out."

But Ivy knew there was no time to waste. "Megan, go back to Viola and tell her I'm with a guest, but I'll get it shortly. And try to keep Lea from going anywhere."

"I'll help with that," Poppy said, putting down her clippers.

"I should tell Mitch I'll be late coming home." Shelly folded her arms. "If that woman makes a run for it, tackle her. Scream, and Sunny and I will come running."

"That's not a bad idea," Imani said quietly. "Poppy, you get out there with Megan and distract them. And Ivy, you need to call Clark right away."

"I'm on it." Ivy knew the thief's trail would grow colder with every passing minute.

With a heavy heart, she dialed the police chief's number. She hated to think the Seabreeze Inn might once again be embroiled in a scandal—and on the day before a grand gala so critical to its future.

18

 he saleswoman flicked her long, manicured nails. "Surely one of these evening gowns would be perfect for your wife."

Bennett stood before an array of glittery dresses, too dazzled to decide. He'd taken off at lunch to drive to the neighboring community that catered to a high-end clientele. He wanted to buy something exquisite for Ivy that she would never agree to otherwise. "She needs a dress fast, but none of these looks like her."

"Maybe not the way she dresses every day, but for one evening, she'll want to shine."

Like a lighthouse, he thought. Reams of sequins, plunging necklines, thigh-high slits, body-hugging. Every dress was pretty revealing. Ivy would feel uncomfortable in any of them.

The woman tried again. "Which one do you think *she* would like?" she asked, her voice a gentle nudge.

Frankly, any of these were better than the disastrous dress he'd seen in her closet. He needed a replacement fast. Surveying the array of sparkly gowns, he tried to imagine her in each one.

Ivy's style was a reflection of her. She would want something elegant, even understated. She didn't need the fanciest outfit in the room to shine.

The woman selected a seductive dress. "Women like classic black because it's very slimming."

"That's pretty far from classic."

"You don't want her to look like your mother."

He ignored her comment, yet the thought of the pink prom dress loomed like a gaudy specter. "Still, they're not quite her. She's hosting an important fundraiser and auction. Many people from San Francisco and the Bay Area high society have flown in for the event."

The saleswoman nodded, understanding dawning in her eyes. "You want her to feel confident, to stand out for the right reasons."

"Exactly." A sense of urgency seized him. "Are you sure alterations can be finished by early afternoon tomorrow?"

The saleswoman's assurance was quick and confident. "Our alterations person is excellent. She'll match the dress you brought as a size reference. That was very smart, by the way. Although a dress can't be returned once it's altered."

Bennett thought of calling Ivy, but he knew what her answer would be. The only way was to surprise her. Even if she didn't love his choice, anything would be an improvement over what she had.

"Do you have someone you can call for a second opin-ion?" The saleswoman sounded sympathetic. "A sister, a best friend, her mother?"

That's what he needed—someone with a keen eye for style and an intimate knowledge of Ivy. Bennett's mind raced. Shelly was too close to the situation; she would tell her sister, and Ivy would insist she didn't need anything. Many of her friends were involved in the gala preparations. But Carlotta, with her impeccable taste, she would know what to do.

"Good idea." He fished out his phone and tapped her

mother's number, hoping she and Sterling were in port and not sailing across the open seas.

The phone rang several times. Bennett wondered if he'd have to navigate this decision alone.

A moment later, Carlotta answered. Her melodious voice, touched with concern, was a lifeline across the miles. "Hello, Bennett? Is everything okay there?"

"Everyone is fine." Bennett heard the background chatter of other people. "You sound like you're on land."

"Not for long; we're in an airport. Sterling and I decided to take a side trip. What's going on there?"

"You know about the gala. Well, I have a situation I could use your help on." Quickly, he explained his predicament. The pink prom dress, the boutique, the sea of dresses, and the dire need for her discerning eye.

"I'm so glad you're doing this," Carlotta said. "The girls sent me a photo that I thought was a joke. Shelly looked lovely, but the dress Ivy had on was utterly atrocious. Sometimes, she's far too practical."

"I can't let her wear that. If you have a few minutes, I can show you some of the choices on video."

"Bennett, you dear man. Of course, I'll help. Show me what you've found."

The saleswoman had overheard and was already ushering Bennett to a quieter corner of the boutique for privacy and better reception. Switching to a video call, Bennett panned his phone across the spectrum of dresses.

"No, no, and definitely not," Carlotta said, her voice firm but not unkind. "We need something timeless. Classic elegance. Ivy should wear the dress, not the other way around. Not twenty-something sexy, but not matronly. Even a silk blouse and skirt, but in the same hue. Something that will skim the body to visually lengthen her petite frame."

The saleswoman, who had been following the exchange, perked up at Carlotta's criteria and disappeared into the back of the store. She returned with a dress that captured the essence of what Carlotta described. It was a subtle black evening dress with exquisite detail.

"This one just arrived," the saleswoman explained. "I haven't had time to steam it yet."

"That's the one," Carlotta declared. "Ivy has pearls that will be perfect with it. Very chic, very Chanel."

"But not the Chanel price tag," the saleswoman added.

"Hold on a moment," Carlotta said, muffling the phone instead of muting it.

Bennett could hear a commotion on the other end. It might be time for them to board.

Carlotta came back on the line. "Get the dress. She has shoes that will match it. You two will have a wonderful time at the gala. We'll call you later."

Bennett felt a swell of gratitude. "I wish you could be here, but we'll send photos and videos. Have a great trip," he said before hanging up.

Bennett handed over his credit card. Relief rushed through him. Ivy would be radiant and feel confident, and that was all that mattered to him.

As he drove back to City Hall, his mind was still on the gala and all the preparations Ivy was overseeing. Just as he pulled into his parking place, he received a text on his phone.

It was the young reporter, Jim Turner. He wanted to meet again, but his time, he said he had different questions. Specifically, about Wyatt and the marina.

Bennett didn't know what Jim was getting at, but he intended to find out. Tapping a quick reply, he told Jim he could meet with him after the gala.

19

*P*ressing a hand to her racing heart, Ivy paced the kitchen floor littered with petals and leaves from the floral arrangement. She swept them aside, clearing a path.

Amelia's vintage necklace had more than a high monetary value; it was the star attraction for the gala and guests. Viola had never parted with any of Amelia's treasures in the San Francisco house, and this was a chance for collectors to own a part of the city's history.

The mood in the kitchen had shifted from one of celebration to one of deep concern. Ivy hated that this had happened. Poppy had joined Megan and Viola in the library to keep a close eye on Lea in case she tried to leave.

Still, preparations for the gala had to go on. Shelly and Imani continued working on the floral centerpieces in the subdued atmosphere. Sunny methodically stripped leaves, snipped stems, and ferried flowers and centerpieces to tables in the ballroom and other parts of the inn. Sunny and Poppy still needed to finish the historical displays in the parlor. They would all be working late tonight, especially now.

Shelly swept an armload of excess leaves and stems into her compost bag. "Once these centerpieces are on the table, we'll add the taller stems and curly willows as finishing touches. We couldn't carry them if we tried to do it all in here." She sipped her cocktail and glanced at Ivy. "How are you holding up?"

"Just wondering how I could have let this happen." Ivy folded her arms, dismayed at the turn of events.

"You can't help it if someone set out to steal that," Shelly said.

Ivy watched a police car pull into the car court behind the kitchen. A uniformed officer stepped out. "We should have had a safe here," she said glumly.

"We should all have a lot of things," Imani said. "But this was not your fault, girlfriend."

Ivy opened the back door to Chief Clark Clarkson, a tall, barrel-chested man. He and Bennett were good friends and colleagues. Ivy greeted him with relief.

"Smells mighty good in here." Clark's gaze swept over the flower-filled kitchen, taking in the situation. As his eyes met Imani's, a smile touched his face. "Nice to see you."

Imani smiled cordially as she arranged roses. "Likewise, Chief. I appreciate your getting out to see my client so quickly."

Ivy knew that Imani and Clark were dating, but they were still professional. She drew a breath, trying to remain calm.

"Mind if I have a word with your client?" he asked.

Imani gestured toward Ivy. "That's what you're here for."

"So, tell me what happened," Clark said, turning back to Ivy.

"The vintage necklace that belonged to Amelia Erickson is gone," Ivy said, reigning in her panic. "Viola Standish is donating the necklace for the fundraiser. We were supposed to display and auction it tomorrow. Plus, we have auction house representatives from Los Angeles coming in to handle telephone bids. This is a huge deal."

As Sunny slammed the kitchen door behind her, Imani stepped to her side. "Can we take this somewhere quieter?"

"In the library," Ivy replied. She led Clark and Imani to the wood-paneled room where they could talk without interruption.

Ivy recounted the details, her voice regaining its steadiness despite her turmoil.

When she finished, the chief nodded with satisfaction. "I'll need to speak to Mrs. Standish now."

"She doesn't know about this yet, but I'll get her." Ivy excused herself. Her stomach knotted at the thought of delivering the news. She made her way to the parlor. "Excuse me, Viola. I need your opinion on something. Do you have a moment?"

Ivy waited until they had returned to the library before she told her the news.

"Stolen? Oh, dear heavens." Shock rippled across Viola's face, and she reached for a chair. "What a catastrophe. Just when I thought we had enough to deal with."

Clark introduced himself. "Ma'am, I'll need to know where you were and if you noticed anything unusual."

As Clark took her statement, he jotted a few notes. "And the two women you were with, Megan and Lea, were they with you the entire time?"

"Why, no," Viola replied. "Lea stepped away to place a call. She was gone about ten minutes."

Ivy rubbed her forehead. *Ten minutes.* Enough time to go upstairs, grab the necklace and jewelry box, stash them, and return to the parlor.

That detail hung in the air among them, heavy with implications. They all traded looks, likely thinking the same thing.

The chief eased back in his chair. "Thank you, Mrs. Standish, that will be all for now. Ivy, would you fetch Lea for questioning?"

"Of course, but first, I should tell you about her." She gave

Clark the thumbnail explanation before walking back with Viola. She didn't want to believe that Lea could be involved, but the facts aligned.

As they turned the corner into the hallway, Ivy nearly bumped into Meredith, who looked fresh from her spa visit.

"What a wonderful recommendation, Ivy." Meredith beamed, unaware of the unfolding drama. "I've been pampered from head to toe, literally. I had a wonderfully relaxing massage, had my hair done, and finished with a mani-pedi." She fluttered her nails.

Viola clutched her niece's shoulder. "I'm afraid we have some rather unpleasant news, dear. Come with us."

Ivy managed a tight smile and escorted Meredith and Viola back to the library, where the tension was palpable.

At the sight of the police chief, Meredith looked stricken. "What's happened?"

"The necklace has been stolen," Viola said. "Right out from under us. And we have our suspicions."

Meredith's face drained of color. "Oh, my goodness, I feel terrible. I should have left it where it was," she stammered, her confusion echoing in the hushed room.

"What do you mean?" Ivy exchanged a puzzled look with Viola. "It was in the hidden room, wasn't it?"

Meredith looked sheepishly at the small group gathered in the library. "Viola, while you were bathing, Betsy called. She's interested in bidding on the necklace but wanted to see how it looked on me. I didn't want to disturb you, so I took it to my room and tried it on for her. I sent her videos and photos. But then, when I went back to your room, the door was locked. I assumed you were still bathing or dressing. I didn't want to disturb you, that was all."

"And where did you last see it?" the chief asked.

"Why, I locked it in my suitcase."

Viola peered at her niece. "Your suitcase?" she echoed, her tone a mixture of disbelief and exasperation.

Ivy pressed a hand to her mouth. The idea that the necklace had been so close, locked away in Meredith's room while they all panicked, was almost too much. She didn't know whether to laugh or cry with relief.

Clark raised an eyebrow but remained composed. "We'll need to retrieve it immediately to ensure it's the same necklace."

In the wake of Meredith's revelation, Ivy's pulse raced as they hurried to her room. Nearly accusing Lea cast a cloud of guilt over her, but the pressing need to see the necklace overshadowed that feeling.

They followed Meredith to her room and watched her unlock her suitcase with quivering hands, lifting the lid to reveal the gleaming necklace nestled amongst her clothes.

"Here it is," she said, gently handing the necklace and jewelry box to Clark. "I'm so sorry. I was in a hurry for my appointment and simply forgot to tell my aunt. I didn't think she'd go looking for it." Meredith's apology trailed off with genuine regret.

Ivy spoke up. "I was the one. Megan and another guest, Lea, wanted to see it."

"That's a popular piece of jewelry," Clark said. He turned to Viola. "Mrs. Standish, if this is the necklace in question, do you have anything you want to add about this incident?"

"That is indeed the necklace," Viola replied in a firm voice. "Chief Clarkson, if my niece meant to steal that, she wouldn't have trotted off to the day spa for hours, would she? No harm done."

Ivy nodded. "May we keep this between us for now? The less drama before the gala, the better."

Meredith carefully placed the necklace back in its box. The necklace was safe, the gala could go on, and the inn's reputation would remain intact, at least for a bit longer.

Viola turned to the chief with gratitude in her eyes. "Chief Clarkson, I'd feel more at ease with you at the gala.

Please consider this an invitation. With your wife, of course."

"Why, thank you, ma'am. I'm not married, but there is someone special I'd like to bring." Clark glanced at Imani.

Imani's response was quick. "I have just the dress," she said, smiling.

Clark grinned. "If you're through with your client, may I escort you downstairs?"

After Clark and Imani left, Ivy carried the jewelry box and rejoined Lea, who had been waiting in the parlor. Viola and Meredith accompanied her.

"That took a bit longer than I thought," Ivy said, still trying to regain her emotional equilibrium. "Here it is." She opened the jewelry box and lifted the necklace.

Lea spoke with hushed awe. "Oh, it's stunning." She held it to her neck and turned to a mirror, smiling wistfully at her reflection. "It's as if I can feel Amelia's presence."

Ivy watched her, the knot of worry in her stomach dissipating. Half an hour ago, she'd thought Lea was the culprit. Now, she felt terrible that a relative and passionate admirer of Amelia's legacy had no means to bid on the necklace. The beautiful piece would probably fetch multiples of Lea's annual teacher's salary at the auction.

If only it were within Ivy's power to gift it to Lea. She was the rightful heir, after all.

While Megan photographed the necklace, Ivy left to return to the kitchen. She walked back through the ballroom, impressed with the floral centerpieces and displays. In the kitchen, Shelly and Imani were finishing the arrangements. Sunny and Poppy were still assisting.

"What a long, wild day," Shelly said, jabbing another hardy stem into an arrangement. "Imani will take me home, and Mitch has dinner ready for us. If I can stay up long enough to eat, that is. I might be in bed before Daisy." She stifled a yawn. "Mind if I leave the Jeep here?"

"Of course not," Ivy replied. "The flowers look beautiful. You've really outdone yourself."

"I had lots of helpers." Her sister shrugged off the compliment, but Ivy could see the happiness in her eyes. "It feels good to know I've still got it."

After Shelly and Imani left, Ivy helped Sunny clean up. She was pleased that her daughter was now pitching in as part of the team. "You've done a lot, Sunny."

"The day isn't over yet, Mom. Poppy and I will finish the historical displays tonight."

"Then I'll call for pizza and salad."

After the full day they'd had, no one would want to make dinner. Ivy expected Bennett home from work soon, but he'd also had a long week. They had made dinner reservations in town for many of their guests, so it would be relatively quiet this evening.

Ivy checked the time and brought out the cheese and appetizer platters she'd prepared earlier for the wine and tea reception. As she was setting up, Viola stopped by the music room.

"What a fright Meredith gave us," Viola said. "I have to apologize again on her behalf."

"I'm glad it all worked out well." Ivy imagined how worried Viola must have been. "I feel bad for Meredith. It was an honest mistake."

"Nevertheless, you did the right thing. For a while, I imagined I'd have to replace that necklace with something of mine." Viola smiled. "At least it would have been a tax write-off."

Ivy appreciated her wry humor. She withdrew a cork from a bottle. "Would you care for a glass of wine?"

Viola hesitated. "Usually, I reserve my wine for dinner, but that was quite the incident. Perhaps a small splash for my nerves. With some of that lovely cheese, thank you. Will you join me?"

Ivy smiled at the elegant older woman. "Just a splash."

After preparing their glasses, Ivy touched hers to Viola's. "To a successful event tomorrow. Thank you for all you've done. Your support means so much to me and my family."

Viola smiled at her over the rim of her glass. "We like to support those who deserve it."

As they sipped their wine, Ivy broached the subject lingering in her mind. "Lea admires the necklace so much. I plan to give her some small tokens to remember Amelia by. After all, she is her only heir. I'll give her the address book we just found; some of those contacts might have living relatives she could look up. We'll also offer her some Christmas ornaments, silver, and any books she wants."

"What a lovely idea," Viola said. "She seems quite nice. If only someone had contacted her earlier." She shook her head, clearly considering the claim Lea might have against the estate.

"I suppose we'll find out soon enough."

Viola nodded thoughtfully. "We had a good talk today with Megan. I'll think about this, Ivy. Amelia would have wanted her to have something special."

Two teenagers from the school music program arrived carrying instrument cases and music. Ivy welcomed them, introduced them to Viola, and they began to set up.

Ivy chatted with Viola a little more before she left to dress for dinner. Watching her go, she wondered what Viola might find to honor Amelia's memory and Lea's deep affection for her past.

Or would Lea serve her and Viola with a demand? Ivy couldn't change the past. In the end, the decision would not be hers. Still, she could commit to having a wonderful time tomorrow.

. . .

Later that evening, Ivy passed by the library where Poppy and Sunny were organizing the historical items for display. It was growing late, and they were finishing their project.

Her daughter's voice floated from the doorway.

"Wyatt shouldn't even think about running for mayor," Sunny said, her voice laced with outrage. "Not with what he's doing."

Ivy slowed her step, listening.

"That was pretty shocking," Poppy said. "I mean, you see that in clubs and read about it, but this guy wants to be the mayor of Summer Beach? I don't think so. We should do something about that."

Ivy stepped inside the door. "I didn't mean to eavesdrop—"

"Mom," Sunny said, looking surprised. "We didn't know you were there."

"What was that about Wyatt?" she asked.

Sunny raised her brow, her youthful face etched with a seriousness that Ivy hadn't seen often. "If he runs for mayor…"

"It's just something we saw," Poppy finished for her.

Ivy felt her heartbeat quicken. "What?" The air was suddenly thick with implication.

"He was doing something he shouldn't have been," Sunny admitted, her voice edged with disgust. "We weren't. We were just there minding our own business."

Ivy's mind raced. "Sunny, if it's something serious, we should talk about it."

"If anyone gets in trouble, it would be him," Poppy said, jumping to her cousin's defense.

Ivy was alarmed, but she needed to stay calm with Sunny. "What happened?"

Sunny picked up a photo. "It wasn't just that... I don't know what to do with all this yet. He told me things that, now that I think about it, sound… unethical."

Poppy flashed her a look.

Ivy approached the pair, her maternal instincts in over-drive. "Are you girls in any trouble?"

"Nothing like that," Poppy said, holding up her hands. "It's a question of what we do with what we know—now that we know Wyatt plans to run against Bennett."

"Whatever it is, you should bring that up to Bennett," Ivy said. "Is it urgent?"

Both young women shook their heads. "It can wait until after the gala," Poppy said.

"I trust you two," Ivy said slowly. "You'll tell me when you're ready?"

"We promise," Sunny said, picking up another photo-graph. "We need to finish this project now."

"Okay, but don't stay up too late. Tomorrow is the big day." Ivy eased the door closed and continued through the house, thinking about what they might have seen and the potential ramifications of their words.

20

On the morning of the gala, Ivy woke early. After leaving Bennett still sleeping, she let herself into the kitchen.

Poppy turned to greet her. "You're up early."

"So are you. Couldn't sleep?"

"I'm too excited." Poppy punched the button on the coffeemaker. "Sunny and I finished the historical displays." She paused a moment. "After breakfast, Sunny and I have to go out."

"That's fine. If you're getting supplies, ask Shelly if she needs anything." Ivy wanted to ask more about Wyatt, but the floors creaked overhead. Guests were already up and moving around.

"Sounds like we have other early risers," Ivy said. "I'll look at the displays after breakfast. And put some of that smoked salmon aside for yourself."

Ivy had created an enhanced breakfast menu for this special weekend. In addition to the usual muffins, juice, hard-boiled eggs, fruit, cereal, and yogurt, she added avocado toast, bagels, and smoked salmon.

"Let's get to work." She and Poppy needed to set up the

breakfast feast.

Ivy opened the French doors in the dining room to let in the fresh morning breeze. She also lit the fireplace at one end of the room to chase the overnight chill. Soon, the sun would warm the rooms with expansive windows.

Sure enough, a couple strolled in a half hour before their usual opening time, but breakfast was ready.

"Good morning," Ivy said. "It's going to be a beautiful day. I lead a walk on the beach after breakfast if you want to join me. I can share some history and ideas on what to do in Summer Beach."

"Sign me up," the man said.

The woman pecked his cheek. "I'll be at the yoga class."

Soon, the room was buzzing with energy, and many people were talking about the evening ahead.

Ivy made her way through the tables, refilling coffee cups. "We have special items for breakfast today," she said, directing guests to the self-serve banquet tables.

Carrying a basket of blueberry muffins, Poppy swept up behind her. "Sounds like the silent auction is getting competitive. People are already bidding. What should we do?"

Ivy grinned. "Let them bid. That's a good thing." She was pleased the silent auction was gaining traction, though they hadn't meant to open bidding yet. People must have seen the bid sheets they put out last night and started early.

Guests meandered in wearing casual hoodies and T-shirts, in contrast to large, glittering diamond rings and expensive watches. This crowd looked more affluent than their usual guests. Ivy hoped they would bid high on the auction items.

She caught snippets of conversation as guests eagerly anticipated the first glimpse of Amelia's Victorian necklace.

What a relief that they had found it, Ivy thought.

She set down the tray of bagels and turned to Viola and Meredith, who were enjoying the avocado toast. "How are your accommodations, ladies? I hope everything is to your liking?"

Viola looked up, her face glowing. "We slept wonderfully with the sound of the ocean so close. And your breakfast buffet is delicious, especially the muffins."

"Shelly's husband makes those for us," Ivy said. "He owns Java Beach and brews the best coffee in town. What will you do today?"

"Someone mentioned a fabulous shop on Main Street that deals in antiques," Meredith said. "We're going there. I hear there are some real treasures."

"That's Antique Times," Ivy said. "Our friends Nan and Arthur own it. They have a wonderful assortment, and they've donated some pieces to the auction as well. The ship captain's wheel in the ballroom came from them. It might be hard to ship home, but it's a beauty."

Meredith laughed at that. "You'd be surprised what I ship from all over the world. I've learned that if you see a unique piece, chances are you'll never see it again. You have to buy it right then."

A younger friend of Meredith's paused at the table. "My husband and I are off to the beach. But first, we'll stop by the auction table. And we want to bid on the African safari trip. The competition is heating up."

"Enjoy the beach. And good luck with your bids." Ivy felt like the day was off to a good start, and Viola made no mention of the potential situation developing with Lea. That was just as well. She couldn't think of that today.

All around her, guests chatted about everything from their plans for the day to auction strategies and what they planned to wear to the gala.

Ivy refilled Viola's coffee, and a guest at the next table leaned in. "I've got my eye on Carol Reston's autographed music sheets," he said. "But I have a feeling I'll need to bid high."

"May the best bidder win," Poppy said, handing him a muffin. "Remember, it's all for a good cause. Be sure to stop by the parlor, where you can learn all about the history of the inn and the Ericksons. You can watch a silent film clip of Amelia Erickson in the library and read what she said. It's fascinating."

The room was a symphony of clinking cutlery, laughter, and the occasional teasing taunts. Ivy moved around the tables, offering refills. She stopped by Lea's table and filled her cup.

"What are your plans today?" Ivy asked.

"I thought I would go for a long walk on the beach and get a massage," Lea replied. She was dressed casually with her hair pulled back. "With my wedding coming up soon, I'm glad to have some time to myself. My life can be quite hectic."

"It's good to pamper yourself and be alone with your thoughts." Ivy smiled at the younger woman. "You probably don't have much time to do that with your schedule." Ivy imagined teachers were just as busy in German schools as they were here.

"Are you excited about the gala?" Lea asked.

"Oh, yes, we're all thrilled," Ivy replied. She didn't sense any underlying motive in Lea's demeanor. "When Viola suggested it, I was amazed. I've been so grateful for my experience here. This old home has gone through several uses already, from its wartime service to its current role—with more to come in the future."

"How is that?" Lea asked, sipping her coffee.

"It will become even more of a destination for community events. We already host young musicians, book clubs, and other meetings. We've had one art show on the grounds and plan on making it an annual event where we'll showcase young artists' works. And a lot more."

Lea listened intently. "We're all here to grow and change,

even old houses. That's a constant in life. We never stop learning."

"I suppose not." To Ivy, the inn was more than just her business; it was her passion. The historical home also meant so much to Summer Beach residents. Whatever happened, she hoped Lea felt the same.

Viola stopped by the table. "Lea, dear. After breakfast, would you have time to visit? There is something I'd like to share with you."

Lea looked surprised. "I'm almost finished here. I could visit in a few minutes if that's convenient for you."

Viola nodded. "And you, too, Ivy."

"Of course." Ivy was ready. After Viola had called her last night, she'd stayed up late getting ready for this meeting.

Upstairs in the quiet sanctuary of Viola's suite, which once belonged to Amelia, Ivy felt the weight of history. She sat with Viola, Meredith, and Lea at a table in front of a window that framed the ocean view. They were high above the activity of the bustling inn.

Even when Ivy lived in this room, it echoed Amelia's charisma. It still did. Ivy shivered as a cool draft brushed past her.

Oddly, she sensed Amelia's presence here more than ever today. Maybe it was because she didn't spend much time here now. That was it, she decided, glancing at Lea. The other seemed not to notice anything.

"I have something I thought you might like to have, Lea." Viola brought out a small velvet box and opened it to reveal a delicate blush-pink cameo necklace.

Ivy watched Lea's eyes widen with admiration. "Why, it's beautiful."

"Amelia wore this in many photos," Viola said, her voice

tinged with nostalgia. "We want you to have it, Lea. To remember her by."

"Thank you," Lea whispered, pressing a hand to her heart. "This means so much to me. I'd love to put it on right now."

"I'll help you with the clasp," Meredith said, smiling. "Even after all these years, the clasp is still sturdy."

"I shall cherish it," Lea said, embracing Meredith and Viola.

Viola looked pleased. "If you will leave your address with us, we have a few other items we thought you might like to have. We can post them directly to you."

"That is kind of you," Lea said happily. "I'll leave it with you."

Lea appeared genuinely touched, Ivy thought. She brought out an envelope of old photographs she had curated.

"You might like to take these with you on the flight back," Ivy said. "These are originals, so you can create a family album of your own. Poppy will copy the rest of the photos in the album for you."

Lea accepted the photographs with reverence. "This means a great deal more to me than you know." Her voice was thick with emotion. "To understand where I came from, how they lived, and the values they held..." She paused, blinking back tears before going on. "To be here, surrounded by Amelia's legacy; why, it's more than I ever imagined as a little girl. Thank you."

"There's more I want to show you," Ivy said. "Remember the hidden room I mentioned when I showed you around?"

Lea's expression was one of genuine surprise. Ivy guided Lea to the hidden room behind the panel in the closet. "Be careful stepping inside." She watched the younger woman explore the secret space with wonder.

Ivy told her how the room was used. "When we arrived,

we discovered this by accident. This was the only entryway to the attic."

"How fascinating," Lea said.

Ivy gestured to a small book. "This little volume holds sketches and fabric swatches of clothes she wore. Everything was made by hand then. I'll take this downstairs to display with the other items in the parlor. Poppy and Sunny arranged some of Amelia's lovely dresses there."

"I saw those this morning," Lea said. "This is all amazing to me. I'm so happy to see it."

After closing the panel in the closet, Ivy led her back into the suite. "Next time you return, we'll put you in this room."

Lea continued to inspect every small item they shared with her. Ivy felt like she was passing a torch, sharing the intimate threads of Amelia's life with someone who cherished them as much as she did.

"Amelia also had quite the library of books," Ivy told her. "We have them downstairs where the book clubs meet. If you see any you like, please take them with you, or we can send them."

Lea clasped Ivy's and Viola's hands in hers. "With you two, Amelia's homes are in the best of hands. I know that in my heart. I believe she would be very pleased."

Another draft touched Ivy's shoulders and she shivered. Was that an approval or admonishment from Amelia?

Viola caught Ivy's eye, a flicker of concern or guilt passing between them.

"Would you like to see the book collection now?" Ivy asked.

A broad smile lit Lea's face. "I'd like that. Thank you all again for these treasures. They mean so much to me, truly." She embraced Viola and Meredith before leaving.

While Ivy walked with Lea downstairs to the lower level, she thought of the tangled web of inheritance and rightful ownership. While she didn't know how the courts would rule, she suspected Lea would have a good case. The mere thought of a legal battle over the inn clenched her chest.

Life was unpredictable, and Ivy knew that well. Sometimes, one had to stand firm, while at other times, one had to flow with the currents of change. Ivy considered the future, the possibility of an out-of-court settlement, or a more personal resolution—however daunting it might be. Now might be her only chance for an amicable solution.

"Lea," Ivy said, her resolve firming. "After the gala, I'd like to talk with you. There's something important that… Well, it could change your life."

Lea's brow furrowed slightly with curiosity. "I'm happy with my life. I'm looking forward to starting a new phase with my husband, but I'm interested in whatever you want to say."

Ivy opened the door to the lower level and flicked on the lights. "It's all down here. Follow me."

Once downstairs, they were alone. Her pulse quickened, and, in a flash, Ivy changed her decision. Instead of waiting until after the gala, she needed to get this off her mind.

She selected words with care. "I'm aware that Amelia's will names your mother as her heir. But no one could locate her. And that means…"

"I'm aware of what it means." Lea looked at her with a calm, unreadable expression.

"Oh. Then we should talk about it." Despite jittery nerves, Ivy tried not to stumble over her words. "About what we should do. I want to see you treated fairly." She waved a hand. "All this should have been yours, so I'm prepared to—"

"Life takes a lot of interesting turns," Lea said, cutting her off. "What you've done means a lot to me. We should talk." She faced the bookshelves. "These were her books?"

Though Ivy had opened the door to the conversation they needed to have, she couldn't read Lea's expression. Regardless, she appreciated Lea's calm response. Maybe she didn't want to create drama before the gala.

Assuming that was the case, Ivy gestured to the bookshelves. "Amelia had good taste in literature. In several languages, it seems. I have to tend to the event, but please help yourself. Or create a stack for us to ship to you. Whatever you want."

"I'll do that." Lea inclined her head. "And, Ivy? I'm glad we're going to have that talk later. After the gala, I think we'll both have clearer heads." With a squeeze of Ivy's hand, Lea excused herself to explore the bookshelves.

Ivy climbed the stairs, wondering how she was going to tell her family this news. Yet, what else could she do but face the facts?

a fter leaving Lea downstairs, Ivy made her way to the foyer. Sunny was there assisting guests with Poppy.

Sunny looked up from the front desk. "Hey, Mom. When are you going to put out your artwork for the auction? A lot of people are checking out the items."

"I'm on my way to my studio right now."

After speaking with Lea, Ivy needed a few minutes alone to recover. Her heart was still pounding from bringing up the subject with the other woman. Her guilt had gotten the better of her. She didn't want something that wasn't supposed to belong to her. *Bad karma*, as Shelly would say.

Ivy wasn't sure why Lea had cut her off, other than it was the day of the gala, and they all had things to do. It would be better to talk after the event.

Sunny arched an eyebrow. "You always tell me not to leave my homework until the last minute."

Ivy gave her a look of surprise. "So, you have been listening to me."

Sunny laughed and hugged her. "Most of the time."

"I'll see you later." Ivy mussed her daughter's thick hair.

178 | JAN MORAN

The love and affection of her daughters, Bennett, and her family was all she really needed in life.

"I know you're busy, Mom. If you set aside what you want to put out at the auction, I'll do it for you."

"Why, thank you, sweetheart." As Ivy walked away, she turned and winked at Sunny. Her youngest daughter was growing up.

The morning light poured into Ivy's studio. Her charcoal sketches of Amelia Erickson and the original Las Brisas del Mar lay on her table.

She had poured her heart into capturing the essence of the inn and its founder, hoping they would resonate with the gala attendees. If people bid on these, she would model paintings for the winning auction bidders after these charcoal sketches.

Stepping back, she assessed her work with a critical eye.

"These need to bring more than just good prices," she said to herself. "They need to tell Amelia's story, to honor her."

She noticed a section on one sketch that she could improve. Picking up a stick of charcoal, she quickly created more definition.

As she was finishing, the creak of the door disturbed the silence. She turned sharply, charcoal stick still in hand.

"We thought we'd find you here," came her mother's warm voice.

"Mom?" A mixture of surprise and joy flooded her. "And Dad, what are you doing here? I thought you were on your boat."

Carlotta embraced Ivy and cradled her daughter's face in her hands, her eyes twinkling. "We needed a break, darling. And what better place than here with you for this special night?"

Sterling appeared right behind her mother. "Give your old dad a hug, too." With his arms held wide, he brought her into a hearty embrace. "We didn't have time to call ahead. Sort of a last-minute decision. Old folks like us sometimes forget to tell the kids what we're up to, right, my love?"

While Carlotta nodded, Ivy melted into her father's arms. "Oh, sure. So old that you're still sailing the high seas by yourselves."

After what she'd just been through with Lea, Ivy was so grateful they were here, but she wouldn't burden them with that story yet. Her parents looked fit and happy, and their noses were slightly sunburned, likely from sailing. They moved with extraordinary vitality; they had more energy than many younger people she knew.

"I'm thrilled to see you, but I'm afraid the inn is all booked up," Ivy said, pulling back with concern. "Sunny and Poppy have doubled up. But you could have our apartment. Bennett and I have camped on the lower level before."

"We knew the inn would be full," Sterling said. "We're staying with Flint."

Ivy was thrilled they were here. "I hope you have something to wear for the gala, because I want you there." While she was having misgivings about settling for the dress she did, it would do. The focus wouldn't be on her but on Viola, as it should be.

Carlotta replied, "I think we might have just the thing."

From the corner of her eye, Ivy saw a shadow flick past the window. The door creaked again, and Bennett stepped inside.

"Hey, what brings you here?" he asked, embracing her parents.

Ivy watched what looked like a practiced charade unfold. Bennett was hardly surprised by their presence.

"What are you all up to?" she asked, her gaze flitting between them.

Bennett reached for her hand. "Come with me to our place. There's something I want you to see."

"But my parents just arrived."

They all laughed. "I promise to bring you back soon," he said. "But you'll want to see this."

Carlotta embraced her. "Go with your husband. We'll follow you."

Ivy was curious as they ascended the stairs. Yet, more than anything, she was happy with the unexpected visit and the chance for her parents to be with family at the gala.

Bennett opened the door to their apartment. "Be right back," he said, dipping into their bedroom. A moment later, he returned with a garment bag and offered it to her. "For you."

"Why, what's this?" Ivy unzipped the bag, her breath catching at the sight of the elegant black dress inside. "Oh, my goodness, it's beautiful. Thank you, darling. It's just what I would have chosen." His gesture was thoughtful, though she knew she wouldn't have time to alter it. The gala was only a few short hours away.

Carlotta clasped her hands. "How lovely. Try it on right away."

Still reeling from the surprise of her parents' return for the gala, Ivy excused herself to humor them.

"I'll zip you up," Bennett said, beaming. He followed her.

She changed and slipped on the evening gown. To her surprise, the fabric fell perfectly over her frame, almost like it was made for her. Even the length looked about right.

Her husband smiled with pride. "Turn around, and I'll close it up."

Astonished at the fit, Ivy held up her hair and looked at herself in their full-length mirror. It fit her so well, she almost cried. "I've never found anything off the rack that fit so well."

"I cheated. I had it altered for you based on another dress you have. We had to guess a little at the length."

"With my heels, it's just right." His thoughtfulness touched her, easing her anxiety over the evening. She smoothed her hands over his broad shoulders and kissed him. "Have I told you how much I love you lately?"

He smiled at her, his eyes crinkling at the corners. "That's a line that never wears out. Use it all you want, sweetheart." With his eyes never leaving hers, he brought her hand to his lips. "You'll be the most beautiful woman there, and I'll be proud to be by your side."

She put a finger to her chin in mock consideration. "Or should I go with the pink one?" she joked, gesturing at the notorious dress that now seemed even more ludicrous in comparison.

Bennett winced at the sight. "Please take that one back. Someone will need it, but not you."

Emerging from the bedroom, she twirled around from her parents. "Well, what do you think?"

"Absolutely perfect," Carlotta said. Her silver bangles jingled as she put a hand to her heart. "Why, I couldn't have chosen better myself."

"No, indeed," Bennett added, a little too quickly.

At that, Ivy figured out what had probably occurred. "Well, whoever was involved in the decision, thank you."

"As beautiful as your mother, you are," Sterling said, his arm around Carlotta's shoulder.

Bennett stepped closer and took her hands. "You look stunning, Ivy. And while I appreciate your thriftiness, sometimes it's good to indulge. As your husband, I reserve that right for you."

She wouldn't argue about the cost now—or at all. "I'll bet you called Mom for help, didn't you?"

Bennett grinned. "I might have had a little help from your mother. They were at the airport, ready to head out on a trip, but instead, they came here to be with us."

The revelation warmed Ivy's heart. "Tonight, we celebrate. Family, legacy, and the future of the inn." Whatever that might be, she'd decided.

The rumble of an engine in the car court below floated through the open door. Ivy glanced outside. "That's the caterer. I'd better change and meet them."

"I'll get them started." Bennett started her zipper for her. "Now scoot."

Sterling held the door for him. "We'll come with you to hunt down Shelly and that cute little sidekick. I'll reckon Daisy has grown a lot since Christmas."

"She's crawling like a chameleon," Ivy said. "Watch out, she's pretty fast."

Carlotta shook a finger at her husband. "See, that's why we need to take more of these breaks."

"This was my idea, wasn't it?" Sterling took her hand, and they set off in search of Shelly.

After they left, Ivy quickly slithered out of the dress and hung it up, admiring it again.

Once back in her jeans and shirt, she hurried downstairs to meet the catering crew.

When Ivy stepped into the kitchen, the aroma of fresh herbs and vegetables filled the air. Chef Marguerite and her team from Beaches were orchestrating the dinner preparations. The catering staff was laughing over something, adding to the pre-gala excitement.

Tonight's menu would include a choice of filet mignon, salmon, or wild mushroom truffle risotto, along with crab bisque, seasonal vegetable salad, and dessert courses.

Ivy watched as the chef, a master of her craft, directed her staff with practiced skill. "Chef Marguerite, seeing you and your team in action is wonderful."

"Thank you, Ivy," Marguerite said, flashing an expression of confidence. "We appreciate the opportunity. We aim to create an unforgettable dining experience." She nodded toward a clutch of young people working in the butler's pantry. "They'll set up the vintage china you wanted to use."

Ivy had thought using what they'd found in the old beach house was fitting. Amelia's refined taste was evident in the delicate patterns and gold rims. The pattern blended well with Shelly's design theme.

"And the retro appetizers we talked about?"

Marguerite smiled. "We're serving Oysters Rockefeller, and pigs in a blanket with Italian sausage. We'll also have shrimp cocktail and watermelon and cucumber-mint skewers."

Ivy was getting hungry already. When the catering team moved to set up in the ballroom, she excused herself for a final review.

She lingered in the grand ballroom, reviewing the transformation and doing a final check. Shelly's floral arrangements brought the venue to life. She had created a floral archway through which guests would enter. Seashells from Amelia's collection were nestled among the blossoms and tumbled across the tables.

The auction table stood ready, brimming with treasures and a growing list of bids that reflected their guests' generosity and competitive spirit. Ivy noticed her sketches were now displayed, and her seascape painting rested on an easel.

The necklace, the heart of the auction, would be the last to grace the table—a jewel among jewels, safeguarded all evening. Chief Clarkson had promised to keep a watchful eye.

She imagined the chandeliers dimmed and the fireplace alive with flickering flames, casting a warm glow over guests. Satisfied, Ivy wound her way through the rest of the house. Candles flickered, lights were lowered, and soft music played.

Sunny and Poppy had created engaging historical displays. Outside, they set out candles in hurricane glasses on tabletops. Once dusk approached, they would light the candles and turn on the lights. The inn's pool was a smaller version of the Neptune Pool, Julia Morgan's artistry at Hearst Castle. The statues added an air of elegance. Shelly had taken care to light them.

Amelia would have loved this. She was pleased with all they had done.

As she stepped back inside, she heard a commotion in the foyer.

The musicians were arriving, carrying their instruments. Shelly was already there to direct them to the ballroom. "You can set up beside the space we left for a dance floor."

Ivy touched Shelly's shoulder. "There's a young pianist, Abby, who will arrive with her mother. She's going to play a song with the musicians, and she's very excited."

Their parents were with Shelly, too. Carlotta was cradling Daisy. The child's tiny fingers reached out, and she cooed in awe at her grandmother's turquoise necklace.

"The event is all coming together now," Ivy said to Shelly.

"I'm so jazzed that Mom and Dad came." Shelly bumped her shoulder. "Think of the funds we'll raise tonight. This old house will get a new lease on life."

"That much is true," Ivy said.

Sterling nodded in agreement. "What you've all done to transform this old beach house into an inn was incredible, but tonight, it's spectacular. You all deserve to soak in every moment of the evening."

Shelly gave her a playful nudge. "Say, shouldn't you be getting dressed, Ivy? Bennett just left, and we've got this covered here. You should be the first to greet people. I'll slip out to dress once you're back."

Ivy's pulse picked up. It was nearly time. "I'll leave you to the finishing touches then."

The walk back to the apartment was short, but to Ivy, it felt like crossing a bridge between two worlds—the chaos of the preparations and the calm before the gala. She closed the front door behind her and exhaled in the cozy comfort of their place.

Bennett was in the kitchen, and she joined him. His hair was wet, and he wore a white terrycloth bathrobe.

"Hey, gorgeous." He enveloped her in a hug and kissed her. "It's almost showtime." Then he tapped a button on an electric kettle. "Thought you might like a cup of tea to relax in your bath."

Ivy loved his kindness and support. "Sweetheart, you're the best, and you've done so much for all of us. Thank you for everything—for the dress, for being here, and for just you."

He took her hands in his. "Seeing you happy means everything to me. Are you sure you're okay? It's been a rough week at times."

"I'm alright." She hesitated, but she had to tell him. She steadied her voice. "Right before my parents arrived, I talked with Lea about the inn. She is aware of Amelia's will and wants to talk after the gala. I imagine we'll discuss this tomorrow."

"And Viola?" he asked, his voice edged with concern.

"I have no idea what she'll do. She called her attorney."

Bennett's brow creased slightly. "Are you sure you're doing the right thing?"

She met his gaze, her resolve clearer than ever. "I am. This feels right, Bennett. It's not just about what I want—it's about what's fair. Maybe Lea could become a partner in the operation of the inn. Or we might create a permanent suite for her and pay rent to her. If we work together, I know we can develop an equitable plan for what we've put into this. She seems reasonable."

"I hope so." He kissed her forehead and swayed with her in his arms. "I trust you'll do what's right. I'll stand by your decision, whatever it is. After all," he added with a smile, "I didn't marry you for your house."

186 | JAN MORAN

"That's a relief." She grinned. "After what you said on our honeymoon, I've been concerned."

Bennett brushed a strand of hair from her forehead. "There's a huge difference between selling the inn to some jerk who'll turn it into a club and making good on an inheritance that should have been hers. How do you feel about giving up what Jeremy left you?"

That was a complicated question, but she'd thought about it. "He earned that money, although he couldn't have done it without my support of our family." She glanced out the open doors on the balcony toward the old beach house. "I figure if I've created one business, I can do it again."

Bennett smiled slowly in approval. "Do you want me there when you two speak?"

His offer warmed her heart. "I'd like that very much." They stood together for a moment, appreciating their partnership in every sense.

"Now, it's time, my love," Bennett said, releasing her hands. "Go have your bath, and I'll bring your tea to you. Tonight, we celebrate everything the Seabreeze Inn stands for and everything we've built together. Our future will be bright, I'm sure."

Ivy kissed him again and went to prepare her bath. Her heart was lighter than it had been in days. In the mirror, she saw the reflection of the woman she had become, and the life she and Bennett had created.

Whatever occurred with Lea, Bennett would be right there beside her. That was all the assurance she needed.

22

"*A*re you ready?" Bennett asked as he slipped on his new jacket.

She paused to admire his new evening suit, which fit him perfectly. He still took her breath away. "Just need help with the zipper."

Tenderly, he swept her hair to one side, zipped the dress, and rested his hands on her shoulders. "You look incredible."

"So do you, darling." Enjoying his touch, she slid a hand over his. "That was an excellent choice. You look handsome in your new suit; you'll turn every woman's head."

"There's only one I want," he replied, nuzzling her neck. "That's the perfume I gave you for your birthday."

"I love it." He'd given her a classic French perfume that was her favorite.

"No one wears it like you." He lingered against her neck. "Need help with your pearls?"

"I'd like that." These small, helpful gestures meant so much to her. Dressing together like this was part of their romance, and she loved it.

Ivy slipped on her heels, and with a last look in the mirror, she was ready.

They went down the stairs, and after they cleared the last step, Bennett offered her his arm.

Ivy slid her hand through the crook in his elbow, her senses prickling with anticipation. The sky was crystal clear, and stars brighten the evening after sunset. She would remember tonight forever.

Ivy and Bennett crossed the patio, admiring Shelly's work on lighting and tabletop decorations as they walked. They entered through the open music room doors, walked past the library, and into the foyer, where Shelly and Imani had added floral arrangements flanking the door. The scent of so many flowers was euphoric.

Mitch stood in the entryway wearing a tuxedo with a Hawaiian print bowtie. His sun-bleached hair rose in perfect spikes. "Wow, you two look incredible."

"So do you." Bennett gave him a fist bump in greeting. "Anyone else here yet?"

"Not yet," Mitch replied. "Shelly just left to help Poppy and Sunny with their hair."

Ivy reviewed all the preparations, making sure that everything was up to the standards they'd set for the event.

Beside the open front door, an elegant, cream-colored sign with gold lettering read: *The Las Brisas del Mar Historical Preservation Gala at the Seabreeze Inn.* A red carpet covered the stone pathway, and valet parking attendants stood ready at the end of the walkway.

"Everything looks ready," Ivy said, satisfied with their work and excited for the evening ahead.

She glanced at the time. A professional photographer would arrive soon to photograph guests. Shelly had created a stunning floral backdrop for photography. Servers stood ready in the ballroom with trays of champagne to welcome guests.

Bennett squeezed her hand reassuringly. "It all looks beautiful, and everything will go well."

"We have contingency plans, just in case anything goes wrong," Ivy said.

Nodding, Bennett added, "I've assigned Mitch to watch Rowan. He'll cut him off if he has too much to drink."

Mitch rocked on his heels. "You won't have to worry about Rowan burning the place tonight." He lifted his phone to take a photo. "Shelly put me in charge of personal photos. Smile." He snapped a few pictures for them.

"Who is watching Daisy tonight?" Ivy asked.

"She's staying next door with Grandma Darla." Mitch grinned. "Those two get along like they're really related. We're lucky Darla adopted us like she did."

"She's fortunate to have you, too," Ivy said.

Admittedly, Shelly hadn't been fond of Darla at first, but when she and Mitch married, she'd set out to burrow under the other woman's crusty exterior and crankiness to find Darla's true heart. The more she was around Daisy, the more often she was caught smiling, and her old wounds were healing.

The musicians began playing, and soon, laughter floated down the stairs. Ivy looked up to see the first guests dressed in exquisite evening wear descending the stairway. She and Bennett welcomed them to the gala, and they passed under Shelly's floral archway into the grand ballroom, exclaiming over the decorations. The heady scent of lilies and roses swirled in the air.

One guest gasped with delight at the sight. "Oh, how lovely," she said. "The floral arrangements are magnificent."

The French doors stood open to the balmy breeze. The setting sun splashed vivid strokes of gold, rose, and violet through the doors and onto the polished parquet floors. Overhead, the chandeliers cast a warm glow, and candles flickered on every table.

The setting was even more beautiful than Ivy had imagined, giving her a sense of how Amelia might have entertained long ago.

Servers stood by with champagne, sparkling non-alcoholic cocktails, and hors d'oeuvres. Shelly had borrowed items from her friend Kai's theater costume department. The servers sported fedora hats and scarves tied at jaunty angles around their necks. They were in the party mood, too.

More guests filtered downstairs, and others staying elsewhere arrived at the foyer. The servers circulated among the guests.

"Look what's happening over there," Bennett whispered, nodding toward the silent auction table. Some guests were hovering near their favorite items as if guarding them. "This could get heated."

"I hope so," Ivy said, smiling. "That would mean more funds for repairs and preservation."

Even the vintage captain's wheel was garnering its share of bids.

Shelly made her entrance in her shimmery watercolor-blue dress. Tonight, she wore her long chestnut brown hair in soft waves.

"You look spectacular," Ivy said. "And you match the decor."

"Just a happy accident," Shelly said with a low whistle. "I heard about your replacement for that pink frou-frou dress. What a relief. You look fabulous."

"Courtesy of my handsome hubby." Ivy hugged her sister, who looked more glamorous than ever. "About time you made it here."

"I was helping Poppy and Sunny with their hair." Shelly turned to the two younger women arriving behind her, clad in pastel colors. "Don't they look marvelous?"

"They do," Ivy replied. "And for once, your hair isn't wild."

"Wait until we start dancing," Shelly said. "Here come Mom and Dad."

The crowd parted for their mother, who looked stunning in a fluid silk aquamarine dress, a statement necklace of silver and turquoise, and an armload of matching bracelets. Her appearance elicited murmurs of admiration.

"Hello, everyone," Carlotta said, her hand resting lightly on her husband's forearm.

Ivy was proud of her mother's unique, enduring sense of style. Just then, she felt a hand on her back.

"Hi, Mom," Misty whispered. "Surprise!"

Ivy spun around to embrace her eldest daughter. "I didn't think you could make it. Weren't you filming on location?"

"The filming is running behind, so my little part isn't until next week now. I came as soon as I found out."

"I'm so happy you're here." With her family around her, Ivy felt the evening was complete.

Around them, the buzz of conversation grew, and laughter and light-hearted banter rose in the air—a prelude to the good-natured competitive bidding to follow. That's what they were all here for—to raise as much as possible for historic preservation.

At a suitable time, Viola made a grand entrance, with Meredith beside her, cradling the star auction item in the glittering, gemstone-encrusted jewelry box.

"The main attraction has arrived," Viola announced, looking regal in a royal blue evening gown. Diamonds and sapphires blazed at her earlobes and throat.

Murmurs rippled across the crowd, and people craned their necks to see the spectacular piece.

Viola stood next to Ivy and faced everyone. "Ivy helped us find this treasure a few months ago. This vintage necklace was given to Amelia Erickson on her wedding day by her dear grandmother. We have an appraisal, but we expect you'll bid even more for its historical value. Megan and Josh Calloway will also feature this necklace in their documentary film. This necklace is truly rare, a one-of-a-kind piece of the finest quality."

Everyone applauded as Meredith opened the ornate jewelry box and placed the necklace under a bright spotlight on a special display stand. The elaborate Victorian-era diamonds sparkled with brilliance under a glass dome that covered both exquisite pieces.

Standing close to Shelly and Mitch, Chief Clarkson surveyed the room with a professional eye. Imani stood beside him, looking beautiful in a one-shouldered, rainbow-hued satin evening gown. Her thick, honey-tinted braids cascaded from an intricate topknot.

Tyler and Celia, Bennett's former neighbors from the ridge, lingered by the necklace. Celia looked chic in an ivory gown. Her jet-black hair was coiled high on her head like a crown, and her elegant, swan-like neck was bare.

Tyler turned to his wife. "The necklace would look amazing on you."

Celia smiled. "I thought you were interested in Carol Reston's handwritten lyrics and sheet music."

"Those, too," he replied. "I want those to inspire the kids in the music program."

Just then, Carol entered in a sweep of burgundy-red sequins, greeting people with air kisses. When she stopped to admire the necklace, her husband Hal shared a conspiratorial wink with Ivy, leaving her with little doubt he would be among the bidders.

On the other side of the auction table, Viola's friend Betsy considered the necklace's potential as a bridal piece for her granddaughter. "Imagine how it would complement Nina's wedding gown."

Ivy scanned the crowd for Lea, finally spotting her standing slightly apart. She wore a simple black dress and a wistful expression. Ivy's heart went out to her. Watching a piece of your history be auctioned off to restore a property you should have inherited must be painful. But tomorrow, they would talk. Ivy hoped they could come to a solution that would benefit everyone.

Once again, Las Brisas del Mar opened its doors for an evening of fun and generosity. Regardless of what happened tomorrow, Ivy would enjoy this magical night.

23

"*We're* at that table," Ivy told her parents, nodding toward one near the front of the ballroom.

The servers had managed to squeeze in more place settings at one of the large round tables. They were family, and cozy was fine.

Bennett ushered her to their seats, his hand steady on the small of her back.

Guests took their seats, and Rowan Zachary sat safely away from the fireplace. Once people sat down, servers placed Chef Marguerite's first course at each setting.

The menu was a hit, from the rich crab bisque and mandarin and avocado salad to the sumptuous main courses. Ivy loved the seared salmon drizzled with a ginger, soy, and maple syrup dressing and topped with caviar. Bennett devoured a tender filet mignon. Sunny and Poppy opted for the wild mushroom truffle risotto, which they said was delicious.

"Dessert, my favorite course," Shelly said, watching the servers. "That rich chocolate ganache with berries has my name on it." She signaled a server. "You can put two of those right here."

Everyone at the table laughed. "*Mija*, I thought I raised you better than that," Carlotta said with a cheerful admonition.

Shelly grinned as the server accommodated her. "You did, Mom. But as the youngest child, I had to fight four older kids for scraps. I'm still hungry."

All around them, the ballroom of the Seabreeze Inn buzzed with satisfaction and anticipation for the auction. When Meredith took to the podium, Ivy sat up to listen.

"The silent auction is officially closed," Meredith said. "I will read a list of our top winners." Meredith read the list of high bidders for each item. When she announced each name, applause broke out.

Ivy was grateful for every donation. Those funds were endorsements of the inn's continued survival. She leaned over to Bennett. "That's a great start on the insulation and window restoration."

Meredith leaned toward the microphone. "For the live auction, we have a special guest auctioneer who speaks at a blazing speed, so you must be quick with your bids. Use your bidding paddle, and for heaven's sake, don't fan yourself with them, or you might find you just bought something, although that's why we're here."

Laughter rolled across the ballroom, and Ivy made sure hers was down on the table.

Meredith introduced the auctioneer, a smartly dressed man. He took her place at the podium.

The live auction commenced, and the professional auctioneer's rapid-fire chant added a layer of exhilaration to the room. He opened the bid for Ivy's seascape painting. Viola and her friend Betsy's generous rivalry sent the price climbing.

Ivy was astonished at the bids. "Bennett, can you believe their bids?" she whispered, filled with gratitude. "I never imagined anyone would pay that price for my work. Surely this is only for the donation or tax write-off."

He squeezed her hand. "Maybe not. You're more talented than you give yourself credit for, sweetheart."

Except for those bidding, a hushed silence enveloped the room. Guests followed the action. Across the room, Lea also watched intensely.

"Now going once, going twice...sold!"

When the auctioneer smacked the gavel, Ivy cried, "Oh, my goodness!" She was astounded by the amount her artwork brought.

Bennett put his arm around Ivy and kissed her cheek. "Congratulations, sweetheart. Your windows will soon be secure."

The artwork was split into lots. Betsy won the seascape painting bid, and Viola nabbed the commissions for the original Las Brisas del Mar and Amelia Erickson paintings Ivy would contribute. Ivy was pleased with those outcomes.

The auctioneer cleared his throat. "The next item up for bid is a two-week Hawaiian vacation offered by Betsy Nightingale at her expansive oceanfront estate on the Big Island. Bidding will begin at ten thousand. That's a steal, folks."

The bids quickly escalated to several times that, and ultimately, Carol and Hal were the winners, much to their delight.

Ivy mentally earmarked that amount for the new roof.

"Next up is an African photo safari," the auctioneer said. "The dream adventure is donated by Teresa at Get Away Travel on Main Street here in Summer Beach. She books trips for people from all over, too. She recently arranged a trip to Mallorca for the mayor and his new wife."

Teresa stood and waved to Ivy and Bennett. Everyone applauded, and Ivy blew her kisses.

"She is such a dear friend." Ivy understood that Teresa

asked her flight partners for hotel and airline donations, and they had come through for her.

A group of Viola's friends snapped up the safari in a heated bidding contest. The sum was another excellent tribute to the cause.

Ivy figured that would cover plumbing, electrical, and so much more.

The room buzzed with chatter and eager anticipation. The auctioneer tapped the microphone. "This is an important one. We have a collection of notated music sheets, hand-written lyrics, and more donated by Summer Beach's Grammy Award winning singer, Carol Reston. These will be sold individually, and Carol is here tonight to pose for photos with the winners."

The auction house representatives took to their phones, providing a conduit to unseen bidders with deep pockets.

The paddles flew, and the bids soared. Tyler seemed determined to claim the collectibles. Triumphant, he claimed most of them, losing only one to a telephone bidder and another to a tech investor friend he'd invited from the Bay Area.

After the bidding closed, Tyler offered his friend more money, but the other man wouldn't oblige. "I'm not here to make a profit off my bid," he told Tyler. "That would have to go to the fundraiser."

Everyone laughed at Tyler's antics. Then, in the heat of the moment, he said, "Fine, I'll double what you paid."

His friend laughed and shook on it. "More money for historic preservation."

"Now I'm in shock," Ivy whispered. Her mother and father hugged her, and her daughters and Poppy beamed at her across the table.

"Just wait until the necklace comes up," Shelly said, winking at her. She crossed her fingers and grinned.

The auctioneer introduced the extra lots of historical

memorabilia that Viola had brought. Those quickly went to the telephone bidders.

The auctioneer held up a hand. "Now we move on to an item of historical significance. A rare, nineteenth-century custom piece in excellent condition." He described Amelia's Victorian necklace in detail, noting the number of diamonds, quality, and so on.

"Based on its hallmarks, this necklace is even more valuable than originally thought. A jeweler to many royal houses in Europe designed this exquisite piece."

Ivy could hardly stand the suspense. She placed a hand over her heart and nodded her appreciation to Viola. As the auctioneer opened the bids, Ivy's breath caught. The room fell silent.

Betsy made the first move with a generous bid that set the pace. Then Tyler and Hal entered the bidding. The auctioneer easily handled rising bids as the tempo clocked like a metronome. The people working the phones lifted a chin or nodded to raise their bids.

At last, the bidding slowed, and Ivy felt faint at the high price achieved.

"Now, going once, going twice," the auctioneer called out.

Another paddle waved the ballroom, and a woman's clear, strong voice rang out her bid. Every head turned in her direction.

Ivy gasped when she saw who was holding up her paddle.

Lea.

How can she do that? Ivy stared at Bennett, who also looked shocked. Murmurs tore through the crowd.

The auctioneer took note. "The bid's in the room. Now, going once, going twice…"

At the back of the room, the representatives on the phone shook their heads.

Ivy held her breath and gripped Bennett's hand. The bids stalled, while Lea's held.

"Sold." The gavel fell with a thud. It was over. "Congratulations," the auctioneer said.

The necklace was Lea's.

Ivy almost leapt from her chair to hug Viola. "I'm so grateful to you for donating the necklace. Your donation will ensure our continued operation for many years to come."

Lea made her way to the podium. On her way, she paused beside Ivy's chair.

Rising from her seat, Ivy said, "I don't know what to say except thank you from the bottom of my heart."

"You've made me so happy, too," Lea said, her face wreathed in a smile. "I'll explain later."

When Lea reached the front, a noise erupted in the rear by the entrance. A tall man had burst through the door and into the ballroom, waving wildly to Lea and shouting something in German.

Reacting instantly, Chief Clarkson rushed toward the intruder. "Sir—"

"Wait," Lea cried, taking the microphone. I know him, it's okay." Her voice sliced through the tension. She held out her hand. "This exuberant man is my fiancé, Michael."

Ivy watched, her mind reeling. With love etched on his face, Michael hurried toward Lea and embraced her. The crowd cheered them on.

Laughing, Mitch called out, "You're too late. She just spent all your money."

"What?" Michael gazed, awestruck, at the necklace Lea had just acquired.

"Look what I bought to wear at our wedding," Lea said, beaming.

Michael took the microphone. "Whatever she spent, fortunately, she can well afford."

More laughter filled the room, and Lea blushed. "I will always be a humble teacher at heart."

Ivy felt grateful, surprised, and relieved. Most of all, she felt deep satisfaction for the gala's success and the future of the property.

Except for dancing and merriment, the nerve-wracking part of the event was over for Ivy. The music began to play, and Carol Reston stepped up to join the band. Shimmying in her bright red dress, she kicked off her set with a spirited rendition of *The Boogie Woogie Bugle Boy*. Ivy knew she planned to sing a few of her most popular hit songs, too.

Ivy beamed at Shelly. "We did it. We can all relax and have a good time now."

"Woo-hoo," Shelly cried, raising her glass. "Let's have fun. Come on, babe." She took Mitch's hand, and they twirled onto the dance floor with others, dancing to Carol's lusty vocals.

Sunny, Misty, and Poppy followed them, along with others their age. Several young men their age asked them to dance.

Chief Clarkson appeared behind them with Imani, and Ivy invited them to sit down.

"Those look like nice men," Imani said, watching Sunny and Poppy. "I'm glad Sunny and Poppy broke it off with that other pair."

Clark turned his gaze on Bennett. "You should be proud of those two. With that video evidence they turned in this morning, Summer Beach won't have to worry about Wyatt and his friend again."

Bennett looked between Clark and Ivy. "I don't know anything about this."

"I overhead Sunny and Poppy talking," Ivy said. "They didn't elaborate, but I knew they had witnessed something disturbing."

"They're good kids, and they did the right thing," Clark said. "Wyatt had big plans for Summer Beach. He aimed to expand his current operation and run drugs through the marina here, among other things. That's what Sunny and Poppy overheard."

"What a relief," Bennett said. "That might be what Jim, the new reporter, wanted to talk about."

Ivy's heart lurched, thinking about how her daughter and niece might have become involved. "I wished they had come to me first."

"They told me they didn't want to worry you because of how important the gala was to the future of the inn," Clark said.

They were right, Ivy realized. She would not have slept a wink.

"Now I'm twice as impressed," Bennett said.

Snapping her fingers with the music, Imani asked Clark, "How about that dance you promised?"

"Duty calls," Clark said before taking Imani to the dance floor.

"That turned out well," Ivy said, feeling grateful.

Bennett looked at Sunny and Poppy in amazement. "They may have averted a disaster in our community. We have to give them credit for that."

Carol Reston segued into another Cole Porter tune, and Ivy watched her family on the dance floor.

She slid her hand into Bennett's. "I can hardly believe this is our life," she whispered, gazing at family and friends around them.

Tonight, it seemed like a dream. It was exhilarating to listen to Carol Reston perform in person, rub shoulders with Rowan Zachary, and mix with wealthy donors who supported her vision of the old beach house as the cultural center of Summer Beach. And the man sitting beside her still made her tingle. She whispered in his ear.

Bennett smiled and swept his arm around her. "I love you, too, sweetheart."

"Here's Lea now," Bennett said, rising.

"Please join us," Ivy said as Bennett shook Michael's hand. "It's wonderful to meet you. How nice that you could join us."

"I wanted to surprise Lea," Michael said. "My flight was delayed two hours, so I almost didn't make it."

"You certainly surprised me," Lea said, beaming. Turning to Ivy, she touched her hand. "I appreciated what you said earlier. You're probably a little confused now, especially since I acquired the necklace."

"I'm still in shock," Ivy said. "I'm sure there's a story behind all this."

"Oh, there is," Michael said. "My soon-to-be-wife is as brilliant as she is beautiful."

"That makes us two lucky men," Bennett added, squeezing Ivy's hand.

Lea smiled at Ivy. "I'll tell you a little now, but I'll save the main story for tomorrow. You see, I had been teaching for several years when I saw a need for software tools to help teachers organize their lessons and have more time for students. I developed this for myself first and later began sharing it with other educators. The application became popular, and I began adding to it as requests came in. My little company grew, and now we distribute educational software across Europe and worldwide."

Ivy listened to her explanation. "That's what you meant by teaching adults now."

Lea smiled modestly. "Yes, and I have more money now than I need. I support other charitable causes, and I am thrilled to be preserving part of Amelia Erickson's legacy."

"It means so much to my entire family," Ivy said. "I'm so grateful for your generosity."

Lea accepted her words with grace. "When we spoke before this afternoon, I was deeply touched by your selfless offer, so I decided to support your efforts. And have a cherished piece of my history, of course. I need nothing besides knowing Amelia's estates are in good hands. I hope we can visit again."

"Anytime," Ivy replied, feeling a kinship with Lea. "But,

please come as friends. Your support means the world to us. I know Amelia would approve."

Lea embraced her. "Her memory lives on in both of us. I'd still like to have that talk tomorrow, but I wanted this little chat so you would sleep well tonight. The inn will be yours for as long as you wish."

24

"*T*hank you for coming to the gala," Ivy said, sending off another guest with a cheerful smile. "Please come back soon to see our planned improvements."

She and Bennett sat at the front desk while Poppy and Sunny handled breakfast. She wanted to personally thank every guest leaving today.

Bennett took her hand. "You looked gorgeous last night. I was so proud of you and all you've accomplished."

"I had a lot of help," Ivy replied, squeezing his hand. "It seemed like everyone had a good time. Sunny and Poppy spent most of the evening dancing."

"We did our part on the dance floor, too," Bennett said, kissing her cheek.

"I love dancing with you," Ivy said, "You have some great moves, sweetheart." Waltzing with her handsome husband under sparkling chandeliers would be a cherished memory.

Fortunately, Ivy had scheduled a cleaning crew early this morning and extended the breakfast hours. By the time most guests strolled downstairs to the dining room, the inn was nearly back to normal. Carpets were cleaned, tables cleared, and dishes washed. To her, that was money well spent.

The French doors stood open to the morning breeze, which swept out stale odors from the kitchen. Chef Marguerite and her team had scrubbed the kitchen after dinner, leaving it cleaner than when they'd arrived.

"Listen to that," Bennett said, lifting his chin toward the dining room. Laughter and light-hearted banter floated down the hallway.

Ivy smiled at him. "The sound of happy guests and the smell of fresh coffee soothes my soul. But I'm going to need another cup soon."

For once, no disasters had befallen them during the gala. No pool rescues, emergency medical teams, or firefighters were needed. The dreaded Mrs. Hampshire, who'd tried to bribe them for a room, hadn't been able to come after all. Rowan Zachary actually behaved himself, aside from fawning over Sunny, who quickly put him in his place. Fortunately, Arlo did not attend with his mother.

Ivy smiled to herself. Sunny and Poppy danced most of the night with a pair of good-looking young men with good manners who were about their age. They were the sons of Viola's friends, and she approved this time.

A couple who had placed the winning bid on one of Viola's auction lots came downstairs. "We thought we'd stroll into the village," the woman said. "Is there anything we shouldn't miss?"

"The sun is out, and it's a nice walk," Bennett replied. "We have wonderful shops on Main Street that are fun to explore. Look for Antique Times, Nailed It, Paige's Books, and The Hidden Garden off Main Street. Java Beach is good for excellent coffee and local gossip."

"I can add to that list," Ivy said. "Past the end of Main Street is the Coral Café, which my friend Marina Moore runs. You can sit on the deck with an ocean view under shade umbrellas. It's great for people-watching, and her food is excellent."

Bennett nodded. "While you're on that side of the village, check out the marina. You'll see many interesting boats. I keep mine there as well. You might run into Tyler and Celia, the couple who won the bids last night on Carol Reston's memorabilia. He's pretty proud of his boat, and it's worth checking out. You can take the beach route back."

"Thanks for that," the man said on their way out the front door.

The people scheduled to check out were gone now. Most guests were staying over and enjoying a long weekend. Chaise lounges near the pool were already filling up.

"Hey, you two," Shelly said as she stepped inside. Mitch was right behind her, carrying Daisy on his shoulders. The little girl squealed with delight when he swept down to clear the doorway. "Have Mom and Dad come by yet?"

"They're in the dining room with Viola and Meredith," Ivy replied. "As it turns out, Viola used to sail. They're plotting a stop in San Francisco to take her out on the Bay."

"That sounds like fun," Shelly said. "Why does it seem like all these retired people are having more fun than I am?"

Mitch bumped her hip with his. "Because they are, babes. You're only as old as you think you are. But now that Daisy is portable, we can get back out there. She'll be old enough to surf with me soon."

"Let's wait until she starts walking," Shelly said. "We want to steal Mom and Dad this morning. They want to spend time with Daisy. We plan to put the floral centerpieces in the Jeep and deliver them to the independent living facility and nursing home here in Summer Beach. I used to do that in New York after the events. Folks there appreciated my work even more."

"The hospital, too," Mitch added. "Though we might have to make another pick-up on the way." He bounced Daisy again. "Come on kiddo, let's go see your other grandma."

"Thank goodness for these high ceilings," Shelly said, her gaze traveling up as Mitch headed toward the dining room.

Ivy leaned on the reception desk, resting her chin in her hand. "I still can't believe how much money was raised last night." It was almost unfathomable, and she still marveled at it.

He clasped her hand. "You'll be able to do all the repairs on your list and have money left over."

"Viola's advisor will help me establish a reserve fund for future preservation." She drummed her fingers on the desk. "What would you think about having an artist in residence program during the off-season? We could also host teachers or scholars who want to do historical research. That would give people a quiet place to write for a week or two."

He tucked a strand of hair behind her ear. "You're always thinking ahead. I like that about you, Ivy Bay."

"Coming from you, Mr. Mayor, that's high praise." She kissed him softly.

Behind them, the stairs creaked, and they turned around.

"Good morning," Lea said. She was with Michael, and the two of them looked happy.

Lea greeted Ivy with double kisses on her cheeks. "Do you have time to talk now? There's so much I'd like to share with you."

"Have you had breakfast?" Ivy asked. "We're serving late today."

"Toast and coffee are all I have in the morning," Lea replied.

Ivy nodded and closed the laptop at the desk. "We'll get that on the way and sit on the patio where we can talk."

While Lea's bread was toasting, Ivy stopped to talk to Viola and Meredith. "What a successful event," she said to Viola. "We appreciate all that you and your friends did."

"That's why friends are so important," Viola said. "Especially at our age."

"We'd love to visit you in San Francisco," Lea said, taking Michael's hand.

"Soon, I hope." Viola nodded. "And you'll stay with us because you're practically family."

Once the toast was ready, they all brought their fresh coffee onto the patio and settled at a table near the beach.

"The sun feels so good," Lea said, rolling up the sleeves of her cotton shirt. "And I could watch that ocean forever." She took a bite of her toast.

Michael stretched his arm across the back of her chair. "Maybe you'll have a chance to do that soon."

"Oh?" Ivy asked, looking between them. "Why is that?"

"I might have a buyer for my company," Lea replied, smiling. "But it's hard to let go of something you've built. We'll see what happens, but first, we have a wedding."

"My mother has planned a large affair," Michael said. "She's done everything. All we have to do is show up suitably dressed."

Lea grinned. "I adore my mother-in-law, and I've been happy to let her do all the planning while I work and travel. I wouldn't have missed this trip for anything. I feel like you're all family, too."

"You're adopted, then." Ivy laughed and tucked Bennett's hand in hers. "But we have many questions first. What did you want to tell me today?"

"I thought you would ask." Lea sipped her coffee before she began. "It was serendipitous, really. I don't have time to read the paper every day, but I was having coffee one day, and someone left one behind. I read an article about paintings that had disappeared during the war and surfaced in California. Most people assumed that artwork had been destroyed. It caught my attention because my grandmother told me about her father, whom she didn't even remember. Family friends told her he'd been the head of a prestigious museum in Berlin. Later, she heard about how he and his daughter tried to save much of the work. Ultimately, he paid the price for that."

"That must have been tragic." Michael rubbed Lea's

shoulder. "The article also mentioned your great-grandmother's sister."

Lea took another sip from her cup. "Amelia, of course. I recognized the name from the old letters my grandmother had given me. I was too young then to ask questions, but I kept them."

"The letters you shared with us," Ivy said.

Nodding, Lea added, "That's how my quest began."

Ivy leaned forward, running her finger around the rim of her cup in thought. "You knew about the will, though. How did you discover that?"

"It was as if the missing puzzle pieces began to fall into place," Lea replied. "I visited the museum where Amelia's father worked. That's where I got lucky. I met a woman who had worked there for decades. Her mother had even worked with Amelia's father during the war, so she had some details. The daughter, much older now, recalled when someone wrote from America, trying to trace Amelia's niece. You must understand how difficult communication could be in the GDR, or East Germany, before the reunification. Those were tough years for my country."

"That must have been the attorney trying to settle the estate," Bennett interjected.

"It was," Lea said, nodding. "She made a note of the attorney's name."

Michael grinned with excitement, still relishing the story. "What are the chances of that?"

"He loves this story." Lea smiled and kissed his cheek. "My grandmother was adopted as a tiny child, but records were sparse, and many were destroyed. The family she lived with were farmers in the country. That's where my grandmother grew up and my mother was born. I spent my first years there until they both passed away, and I was adopted as a child by a family in Berlin. You might say I came full circle."

"When you contacted the attorney, what happened?" Ivy

asked, wanting to know every detail of the story she had long wondered about.

"First of all, the lawyer was no longer living," Lea said. "His son had taken over the law practice. My story intrigued him, so he researched their old case files." She paused to finish her toast.

"Which must have led to your discovery of the will and the properties she left," Ivy said, leaning forward with interest.

Michael chuckled. "The attorney thought she wanted to claim her inheritance. He was very distressed."

"I can imagine," Bennett said. "I worked with the trustee that managed the property for years while they waited for the stipulated time to pass."

Lea shook her head. "By then, my company was doing very well, and I didn't need an inheritance. Why upset what had already been done? Still, I became so immersed in the Summer Beach story and how it related to my family that I read everything I could. I had search alerts set up, and one day, a press release announced the gala and the auction of Amelia Erickson's necklace."

"We booked a ticket for her that night," Michael added. "Finding a connection to her family and ancestry was important to Lea. And someday, it will matter to our children."

Ivy reached for Lea's hand. "Thank you for sharing all of this."

"You haven't heard all of it," Michael said. "Lea called me and told me about Ivy's generosity."

Lea squeezed her hand. "I could see how troubled you were. I knew you wanted to be fair and do what you thought was required. Most people would fight me if I tried to claim the inheritance. But this is your home, so I decided to help ensure you could stay and look after Amelia's legacy. I have another life to live, but your courage inspired me to make that bid."

Ivy was at a loss for words. Bennett put his arms around her in comfort.

"The necklace will be beautiful with my wedding gown," Lea added, smiling at her fiancé. She turned back to Ivy. "This is why I was meant to see that newspaper article that day."

As Ivy looked into Lea's soft brown eyes, she felt their separate worlds tilt into alignment. "There must be a force greater than ourselves that pulled us together," she said quietly. "We have much to tell you as well. Since moving in, we have discovered so much about Amelia and Gustav. And we keep discovering things, like the address book I gave you."

"Which I will definitely go through," Lea said.

"These walls might hold even more secrets," Bennett said. "Wait until they hear what we discovered on Mallorca."

"If you'd like to join us this evening, we can tell you over dinner," Ivy said.

Bennett raised his brow and grinned. "I wonder if the Erickson story will ever end?"

As he spoke, a shadowy movement by a stone wall drew Ivy's attention. She almost swore she saw something. But no, she didn't believe in Shelly's ghost stories. She blinked, and whatever it was disappeared. Ocean mist, perhaps.

But just in case, she murmured, "Thank you."

Lea looked up, too, following her gaze, her lips slightly parted. Then, catching Ivy's eye, she smiled as if they shared a secret. "I suppose we should go now. Michael wants to see Summer Beach, but we would love to meet you for dinner."

After Lea and Michael left, Ivy turned to Bennett. "Are you up for a walk on the beach? After hearing her amazing story, I need a few minutes to take it in."

"So do I," he said, helping her with her chair.

They strolled across the patio. Shelly's floral arrangements still brightened the tables. When they reached the edge of the patio, they left their shoes there. Bennett rolled up his trousers, and Ivy pinched a fold of fabric, lifting the hem of her dress. They stepped across the soft sand toward the water's edge.

In the distance, sunlight spilled across the brilliant blue sea, catching the waves and sparkling like diamonds.

"Would you look at all this?" Bennett said, sweeping his hand toward the horizon.

Ivy gazed across the ocean. "What's out there is so vast that it makes anything in our small part of the world seem possible. That's a lot like love."

Bennett wrapped his arms around her, swaying to the sound of the waves. "You make me feel like that, darling."

"So do you, my love." Ivy rested her head against his chest, feeling his heartbeat.

Life could be complicated, but not their love. It was the constant in their lives now, as strong and sure as the waves that kissed the shore. She raised her face to meet his lips, their souls melting into the place where they felt as one.

Thank you for reading *Seabreeze Gala*, and I hope you enjoyed attending the social event of the season.

NEXT: Read *Seabreeze Library*, the next in the Summer Beach series. A new guest arrives at the Seabreeze Inn, and the Summer Beach library is at the center of a new threat.

BONUS! Discover more in Summer Beach. Download your free Summer Beach Welcome Kit now!

https://janmoran.com/SummerBeachWelcomeKit

Here's what's inside your free Welcome Kit:
• Family Trees – Who's who in town
• Summer Beach Map - Discover the village
• VIP Shopping Coupon – Take 10% off in my online shop
• Printable Book List – A checklist with ISBN codes for booksellers and librarians
• Printable Bookmarks – A fun DIY project
• Recipes – Cool summer refreshments
• Book Summaries – Learn more about each book and where to find them

You'll soon meet folks you'll think of as friends. Read on and find out why readers say, "Life is better in Summer Beach." Enter your email address to receive your bonus scenes by email. (If you don't have access to a computer, ask a friend to print these for you.)

SHOP: Keep up with my new releases on my website at JanMoran.com, and don't forget to shop exclusive ebook and audiobook bundles, coffee mugs, and bookmarks ONLY on my bookshop at store.JanMoran.com.

JOIN: Please join my VIP Reader's Club there to receive news about special deals and other goodies. Plus, find more fun and join other like-minded readers in my Facebook Reader's Group.

MORE: Want more beach fun? Check out my popular *Coral Cottage* and *Crown Island* series and meet the boisterous, fun-loving Moore-Delavie and Raines families, who are always up to something.

Looking for sunshine and international travel? Meet a group of friends in a series all about sunshine, style, and second chances, beginning with *Flawless* and an exciting trip to Paris.

Finally, I invite you to read my standalone family sagas, including *Hepburn's Necklace* and *The Chocolatier*, 1950s novels set in gorgeous Italy.

Most of my books are available in ebook, paperback, hardcover, audiobook, and large print. And as always, I wish you happy reading!

RECIPE: MANDARIN ORANGE AND AVOCADO SALAD

This sunny salad is a favorite among my guests for its fresh, vibrant balance of creamy avocado, crisp greens, and juicy mandarin orange slices. In *Seabreeze Gala*, this is a quick family favorite enjoyed with shrimp right off the grill. The citrus dressing is light and flavorful.

For an easy spring or summer meal, I often add pair with tomato-basil soup, crab bisque, or another light soup. To add more protein, add grilled or pan-seared shrimp or salmon prepared with garlic, olive oil, oregano, and pepper. A side of sourdough bread and a bottle of your favorite white wine will complete this fresh, easy meal.

Macadamia nuts add sweet crunch and a tropical accent, or you may substitute slivered almonds, pistachios, or pecans.

About avocados: Be sure to select creamy avocados (not the light green, think-skinned, watery type—unless you prefer those). In Southern California, the dark, bumpy-skinned Haas avocados are the most readily available. Large Reed avocados are also creamy and delicious; these are often found at farmer's markets and in friend's yards. Similar types are found in Spain and elsewhere. I am very particular about my avocados, especially for this recipe.

If your avocados are not ripe, place them out on the counter until they ripen, which means slightly soft to the touch. Too soft, and they will taste vinegary. Too hard, and they will lack flavor. If the fruit ripens faster than anticipated, put them back in the refrigerator to preserve them until needed. The fruit usually takes about three days to ripen once removed from the refrigerator, so I keep quite a few on hand and cycle out as I plan to use them. If they overripen and go too soft, salvage them for use in guacamole or avocado toast, unless the taste has declined.

Serves 2

Ingredients:

Salad:

4 cups spring mix (about 120g)
1 large avocado, peeled, pitted, and sliced
2 mandarin oranges, peeled and segmented
1/2 cup strawberries, sliced (about 75g)
1/2 cucumber, sliced (about 120g)
1/4 cup macadamia nuts, roughly chopped (about 30g)
1/4 cup feta cheese, crumbled (about 30g)
1 small sweet yellow pepper, sliced

Citrus Salad Dressing:

1 tablespoon white wine vinegar (about 30ml)
1 tablespoon fresh orange juice (preferably from mandarin oranges) (about 15ml)
1/2 tablespoon fresh lemon juice (about 7.5ml)
1 teaspoon honey or agave syrup (about 5ml) (or avocado or olive oil for less sweetness)
Salt and pepper to taste (adjust according to taste)

Garnish (optional):

Fresh mint leaves
A sprinkle of sesame seeds or poppy seeds

Instructions:

1. Prepare the Dressing:
In a small bowl, whisk together white wine vinegar, orange
juice, lemon juice, honey (or agave/avocado oil/olive oil), salt,
and pepper until well combined. Taste and adjust the
seasoning as necessary. Set aside.

2. Assemble the Salad:
In a medium salad bowl, gently toss the spring mix with the
sliced Haas avocado, mandarin orange segments, cucumber
slices, strawberry slices, and sweet yellow pepper slices.
Add crumbled feta cheese and chopped macadamia nuts
on top.

3. Dress the Salad:
Drizzle the citrus salad dressing over the salad, ensuring an
even distribution.
Gently toss the salad to ensure all the ingredients are lightly
coated with the dressing.

4. Garnish:
Garnish with fresh mint leaves or a sprinkle of sesame or
poppy seeds.

Serving Suggestions:

Serve the salad immediately after dressing to preserve the
freshness and crispness of the ingredients.

This salad is perfect as a light, refreshing meal on its own or paired with your favorite grilled protein for a more substantial dish.

ABOUT THE AUTHOR

JAN MORAN is a *USA Today* and a *Wall Street Journal* bestselling author of romantic women's fiction. A few of her favorite things include a fine cup of coffee, dark chocolate, fresh flowers, laughter, and music that touches her soul. She loves to travel, and her favorite places for inspiration are those rich with history and mystery and set against snowy mountains, palm-treed beaches, or sparkly city lights. Jan is originally from Austin, Texas, and a trace of a drawl still survives, although she has lived in Southern California near the beach for years.

Most of her books are also available as audiobooks and have been translated into other languages, including German and Italian.

If you enjoyed this book, please consider leaving a brief review online for your fellow readers where you purchased this book or on Goodreads or Bookbub.

To read Jan's other historical and contemporary novels, visit JanMoran.com. Join her VIP Readers Club mailing list and Facebook Readers Group to learn of new releases, sales and contests.